I0738528

The Secret Diary

of

Francis Lovell

DAWN WHEELER

Just A Thought Publishing
Michigan, USA

Also by Dawn Wheeler:
The Hypnosis I Know

The Secret Diary of Francis Lovell
Copyright © 2019 Dawn Wheeler
ISBN: 1-7330117-0-6
ISBN-13: 978-1-7330117-0-9

Just A Thought Publishing
Michigan, USA

Cover Image - The Order of the Garter stall plate for Sir Francis Lovell, Viscount Lovell of Titchmarsh from St. George's Chapel, Windsor Castle. Reproduced with the permission of the Dean and Canons of Windsor.

This is a work of fiction. Although the characters depicted in this book have actually lived over 500 years ago and some of the events and facts presented are true, this story is a product of the author's imagination. Sadly, no such diary has been discovered as of yet.

DEDICATION

This book is dedicated to the many unsung heroes and loyal friends throughout history. They did what they did, not for glory, nor material or financial gain, but because it was who they were. To these noble men, women and children who did what was honorable and right even if it was hard, I thank you and wish you peace.

ACKNOWLEDGMENTS

To my proofreaders and historical sounding boards extraordinaire, Marie, Philip, Caroline and Tony - Thank you for your time, feedback, support, insights and love of reading and history.

To my wonderful husband Philip - Thank you for your love, support, wisdom and humor, and being who you are. I love you.

PROLOGUE

J ust outside of Oxford England, an ordinary man made an extraordinary discovery. Gerald Dewhurst, antiquities shop owner and Richard III enthusiast practically choked from the shock of what he uncovered in his store's cellar when doing a long overdue cleaning. Buried beneath a pile of boxes, resting inside a well-worn trunk, lay a stack of parchment bearing the name of Francis Lovell.

"It can't be," he whispered, shaking his head, while his now trembling hands gently flipped through the fragile pages.

Gerald stared incredulously at the age worn paper, as he quickly recognized that the entire document was written in some form of old English. It was also clear that every word was formed with a quill versus some modern writing implement. Gerald's heart sped up with excitement as he contemplated the potential authenticity of his find.

He scanned for any familiar words and phrases hoping he would see something that would validate his suspicions. Many names and expressions caught his attention, but most notably of all were references to Minster Lovell and a chamber. Gerald shakily arose from his seated position on the floor, holding the curious pages close to his chest like a precious child. Unable to contain his happiness and nervousness any further he started to laugh. It was a deep from the belly kind, which seemed to get louder as the minutes went by.

"My God, it's true!" he finally shouted amidst his seemingly endless giggling. "It's true!"

With the exception of football matches or competitions at the pub, Gerald was not typically boisterous in his behavior or prone to yelling. Making a potentially significant historical discovery, however, definitely ranked as a celebration worthy moment. He just wanted to shout it to the world.

"It may not be like finding Richard III's bones in a parking lot, but it's bloody close!" he proclaimed out loud.

Gerald continued to shriek and laugh like a fool, all the while staring at his wondrous find. He then made a mental note to contact the Richard III Society about his incredible news.

Gerald's enthusiasm and volume eventually caught the attention of his wife Hannah who was tending to things upstairs. She practically ran down the steps to search for her husband to see what had him so excited.

"What in heaven's name is going on? Why are you shouting so?" she asked, while staring at her giddy husband for some clue.

In the 25 years she's been married to him, Hannah only saw that smile on Gerald's face three times. Once, on the day they wed, then twice more when she delivered their two children.

"What has happened?" she asked again, wondering why he still hadn't answered her but continued to grin from ear to ear.

Finally getting his voice back, he explained rather matter-of-factly, "It's real and I have it."

He looked at her as if she was supposed to understand what he was talking about. She smiled at her dust-laden husband and spoke as slowly and softly as she could. "Dearest, I will need a little bit more information than that."

Gerald cleared his throat and then declared, "I believe I have in my possession a secret diary of

Francis Lovell. A diary I think he may have written in a chamber at Minster Lovell."

"The same Francis Lovell who was King Richard III's dear friend and high-ranking councilor?" she asked, making sure they were on the same page.

"Yes indeed," he said, still smiling.

"The Minster Lovell whose ruin is a mere twenty minutes away from our shop and also happens to be the rumored final resting place for Francis Lovell?"

"The very same."

Before assuming her one and only true love had lost his mind, she decided to give him the benefit of the doubt. Hannah also thought it prudent to see for herself before coming to any conclusions. After asking him if she could take a look, he cautioned her to be careful as he handed over the delicate document.

It was clearly old, how old she could not say, but her curiosity was certainly piqued. Just as Gerald had done a few minutes earlier, she scanned through the pages as gently as she could. She noted everything he noted and more, and now understood completely why he was so excited. After carefully placing the document on the tabletop beside her, she drew her happy husband into her arms for a well-deserved hug and kiss. Hannah then led him up the stairs to make some tea and calmly discuss how to go forward.

To know for sure, they would need to have the document undergo testing and also be translated. And that's exactly what they proceeded to do.

So why is finding a document allegedly written by someone named Francis Lovell significant? Francis was an important but mysterious figure in England's history. His disappearance without a trace fueled the curiosity of many people and incited rumors and legends that to this day beg to be proven or disclaimed. If the stories are true, he wrote down something before he died that might solve some of the greatest mysteries regarding his friend and king, the much-maligned Richard III of England.

Lovell seemingly vanished in 1487, after attempting to overthrow Richard III's successor Henry VII in the Battle of Stoke. Henry's reign was not a result of the natural progression of being next in line to rule. But rather, he took it by force after he defeated and killed Richard in the battle of Bosworth two years prior to Stoke. Understandably, Francis and others who were still alive and loyal to Richard were highly motivated to put an end to Henry and take back the throne. Unfortunately, their efforts failed and Henry and his crown persevered.

For more than five hundred years, the mystery of what became of Francis has both perplexed and fascinated many a history buff. Most people suspected that he died at Stoke or soon thereafter. However, no remains were ever found.

Although no one really knew what happened to him, theories abound regarding his potential survival or demise. Adding to the intrigue is the fact that Francis was equally elusive in life as he was in death. Despite him being one of the most powerful and wealthiest men of his time, very little is known or documented about him. Had it not been for something that occurred long after he and his contemporaries were gone from this world, his name could have easily been forgotten.

More than two hundred years after Stoke in 1708, amid renovations, workmen allegedly discovered a hidden chamber beneath one of Lovell's family estates at Minster Lovell near Oxfordshire. Inside, they found a skeleton of a man sitting at a table, upon which rested a book, a candle, a stack of paper, a quill and an inkwell.

Those present at the time, claimed that within an instant almost everything in the room including the skeleton and document was rendered to dust. The supposed magic like, disappearing phenomena left no trace or potential to identify the person in question or examine his last written words.

Many hypothesize that the sudden introduction of air to the long-sealed chamber was to blame for the shocking annihilation of evidence. Regardless of how or if any remains disappeared, people tend to be more curious about their potential identity. The prevailing assumption was that the disintegrated pile of bones belonged to Francis Lovell himself.

There is much speculation as to how he would have come to stay there and what he might have written before he died. Of the numerous variations, the most common belief has poor Francis accidently locking himself inside this room and starving to death.

For centuries, the musings of the supposed last occupant of the alleged chamber at Minster Lovell were presumed to be lost forever. But now with the Dewhursts' recent discovery, this mystery may finally be solved and prove what many assumed to be a well-crafted tale may actually be true.

Initial testing has suggested that the paper and ink used are consistent with those commonly found during the reign of Richard III. Specific references to a chamber at Minster Lovell and other details pertaining to Francis and the times in which he lived are equally compelling. When combined, it leads many to believe that this alleged historical find could be authentic.

The Dewhursts offer the following translated secret diary of Francis Lovell, and leave it to its readers to decide what truth if any it reveals.

1

HOW SHALL I BEGIN?

They called me the Dog[1]. It was meant as an insult, but I did not take it as such. My support of the king was not out of blind obedience. I did not seek his favor in hopes of having him toss scraps my way. Nor were my actions some contrived scheme for self promotion despite the honors and responsibilities he ultimately bestowed upon me. I was simply a loyal friend.

Our friendship has seen the best and worst of times. Unfortunately, as I sit here today putting ink to paper, I am sad to report that these are the darkest

---

[1] The dog is in reference to the now infamous rhyme written by William Collingbourne, an opponent of King Richard III. He posted his words on the doors of St. Paul's Cathedral in an attempt to mock the king and his closest advisors. "The Cat, the Rat and Lovell our Dog, Ruleth all England under a Hog." The cat represents William Catesby, the rat, Richard Ratcliffe, the hog, King Richard III and our dog is obviously Francis Lovell.

days yet. My friend and many others with whom I have fought alongside are gone. I have spent the last two years since my dear friend and king's death, trying to overthrow the usurper[2] who killed him and took his crown.

Many believed that our last attempt would be successful, but alas, it was not meant to be. Though I survived while others perished, I barely escaped with my life and the secrets I bear within me. Both my body and spirit are in desperate need of rest and mending. My enemies would see me tortured and killed for what I know. Because of this very danger and the poor state of my body, I had no choice but to go into hiding.

It is my deepest hope that honor and reason will once again prevail across the land. But until such time, I shall wait and pray. I hope that I may live to rectify the libelous spewing and unlawful rule of my enemy. Should I perish before this wrong is righted and I can move about freely, let these words I have written bring truth and justice in my absence.

Many presume that I am dead, yet they will never find my body. I pray they do not search too long, that

---

[2] Someone is branded a usurper if they take over another's position of power by force or without legal authority.

I may live to tell this tale. One might consider my choice of hiding places to be a sign of arrogance or some indication that I have gone mad. Others might suppose that I have a death wish. The truth is, I have chosen my refuge with a fairly sound mind and a surprising desire to go on living, even if my body has other intentions.

It is widely believed that I have spent very little time here at Minster Lovell, one of my family's many estates. Those who perceive this to be true also assume that there is no one left here who would remember me, let alone help me.

The manor was recently granted to Jasper Tudor, the uncle of our current king and my sworn enemy Henry Tudor. Given my perceived increased danger and lack of support, most people would view this as the least desirable location for me to bide my time. Yet to me, it seemed like the perfect choice.

Because no one would foresee any logical reason for me to be here, this should be the very last place anyone would look. If, however, someone decides to search the estate, I have taken a few measures to avert their suspicions and prevent my discovery. In fact, the chamber in which I spend most of my time is so well hidden, I am certain they will never find me. I suspect my departed friend would find my location characteristically humorous and unsurprising were he alive today.

I am a poet, philosopher, dreamer and lover at heart, and am best suited for tasks that require administering or organizing. Yet due to circumstances beyond my control, I became a warrior.

To survive the nasty business of war, one must become adept in anticipation and strategy and remain vigilant to stay ahead of the enemy. Faith can push us on in the most troubling of times. But more often than not, it is one's sheer determination and fear that will bring them to victory or lead them to defeat.

I consider myself a practical and logical sort of man. But when the world is in chaos and darkness, and there is no one you can trust, a deep core need to release some anger takes over.

Rage however, seldom solves problems and often makes things worse. Yet if someone is lucky enough to be successful in finding some measure of calm or peace in expressing it, generally it will not be enough or last. Eventually, one must retreat and reassess if they wish to live to fight another day or perhaps determine a new path for their future. Thus, here I sit penning a diary of sorts, as I reflect on what has led me to this point.

I imagine dearest reader that you may be anxious to learn how I was able to flee undetected from my last battle. While I fully intend to explain how I made my way to my current and hopefully temporary residence, I feel the need to discuss other matters first.

2

A DOG'S LIFE

I learned early on that we are but pawns on a chessboard. It is an illusion that any of us have any real say in our lives. A person's birth order, legitimacy, gender, social status and wealth have a more significant influence on one's path rather than their intentions, abilities or deeds. As you can imagine, having to live under such circumstances inevitably breeds jealousy, fear and an unhealthy desire for power.

Power can certainly be earned, but it can also be taken. Those desiring to obtain or hold onto power frequently use others or engage in some manipulation to gain an advantage. Unfortunately, if someone becomes desperate enough, they may not stop there. All too often, I see people consumed with fear and greed going to more extreme lengths to ensure that nothing and no one gets in their way.

Aside from fostering uncertainty and an obsessive need for control, society's power and class oriented structure also shapes the very concept of what a family is and how it functions. Families are rarely ideal even under the best of circumstances. But if you factor in the impact of social order, what can result may be even more disappointing.

Each level of society has its own set of priorities, expectations, opportunities and challenges that influence how family members communicate and behave with one another.

Aristocrats, for example, are commonly lacking in all matters that involve emotional expression and connection. Children, for instance, are regarded by most of the gentry as something to which they can pass along titles or land. Many also view their young offspring as possessions they can broker in order to gain power or wealth. Any potential for bonding is usually thwarted early on.

Lowly wet nurses, nannies, tutors and housekeepers typically nurture the youth of nobles rather than their own mothers and fathers. In my own experience, the maids who took care of me gained more of my affection and were of greater importance to me than either of my parents. I know this may seem harsh, but this is a typical reflection of our times and place in society.

Those who are born into families of great wealth and power receive little to no emotional guidance, warmth or support for surviving life experiences, let alone flourishing. They are also generally discouraged from making their feelings known to anyone, especially children.

The privileged are instructed in what is deemed necessary to carry on as others who came before them. For those wishing to maintain their position in society and hold onto their wealth and property, there can be no room for frivolity or emotional consideration.

Love, demonstrations of affection, or playful or meaningful connection, for example, is considered a costly distraction that people should avoid. Constant fear from frequent political upheaval and war only strengthens the need to stay vigilant and keep one's feelings under control. Anyone would be reluctant to let one's guard down or give in to sentimentality in such precarious circumstances.

As for my own mother and father, for the narrow span of years that I had them in my life, they always seemed preoccupied and distant. Moreover, despite how very young we were, they were definitely not focused on my siblings or me.

It is difficult to imagine what it might have been like had my parents actually doted on me or shared my life in a more deep and meaningful way. Aside from providing some of the necessities of living, they unfortunately were not capable of anything more.

Just like others in my level of society, I was raised as others who came before me. And as others before us, we had to accept our circumstances whether we liked them or not.

Barely out of the nursery, most boys are sent away from their homes and what little comfort or familiarity they have, to begin training in the art of war and the code of chivalry. Those who are not destined to defend king and country may choose to pursue scholarly avenues or serve God.

While their male counterparts may spend their days wielding weapons or contemplating academic or spiritual aspects of existence, female offspring occupy their time with activities that fulfill another set of priorities. Girls are generally raised to be obedient and unobtrusive when interacting with men. They are also tutored in a variety of disciplines that will ultimately help them carry out their duties as wives and mothers.

Although a woman may grow to oversee the running of a household, her greatest importance lies in her ability to produce an heir. Of course, if she is not keen to marry and help continue the family line, she will always have the option of becoming a nun.

While many restrictions and expectations are imposed upon the noble youth, especially the females, the same could be said of those who have come of age. No matter how old one gets, there always seems to be someone telling them what to do, with little regard as to how they may feel about it.

Obviously, constraints and challenges are not limited to the privileged. Those with little to no means or authority experience even greater unfairness on a daily basis. However, from what I have seen, they tend to complain a lot less than those who have more than they do.

I have also observed that despite their greater challenges, the lower rungs seem to have more love, connection and warmth compared to their upper class counterparts. As such, they appear better equipped to counteract or at least better comfort themselves from the unfortunate aspects of their reality. They may disagree. I may be wrong. It is just something I believe to be so.

As for the world of the rich and powerful, I cannot say with certainty that it is totally devoid of all warmth, love or compassion. What I can tell you, however, is that emotional expression is rare and often well hidden from public scrutiny. In those unusual instances when it does happen, affection and more meaningful interaction most commonly occur among friends. Sadly, true friends are often difficult to find.

Thankfully, despite my otherwise unhappy circumstances I was able to find one of my truest friends as a mere boy, a few weeks before my ninth birthday.

Soon after losing my father, I suddenly found myself the ward of King Edward IV. When someone becomes the ward of another, his or her protection and care become the responsibility of their guardian until they come of age. Protection and care are relative, especially depending on who is providing it and why.

No matter how noble it may sound, these types of arrangements rarely occur because someone steps forward in a time of need simply out of the goodness of his heart. There is usually some hidden agenda or motivation or even compensation related to taking on a ward. This is especially the case when the guardian is a virtual stranger versus a family relation.

As for the ward, the alleged protection and care he or she receives often comes with a steep price. A guardian will have complete control over their ward's material goods, properties and financial holdings. They will also dictate every aspect of their ward's life. A ward is expected to do as their designated guardian asks, even if it is the very last thing they would wish to do. Lacking access to that which belongs to you and having no true say in your life until reaching your majority is a high price indeed.

Given the obligation they have taken on, guardians feel justified in being able to impose great restrictions and demands upon their charges. They also expect and frequently receive some relief or benefit for carrying such a burden. As a result, guardians can be gifted or choose to just help themselves to the revenues, property and other resources that will come under their jurisdiction.

My own guardians shamelessly helped themselves to my family's wealth time and again, and made me fight for years even after reaching my majority for what was mine. Guardians will do as they wish regardless of how unfair it may be for their wards. Wards are nonetheless expected to be grateful. Truth be told, despite understanding the reality of my circumstance, I found it very difficult to be grateful.

I was far away from everyone and everything I knew, and there was nothing I could do about it. My family's holdings were inaccessible to me, and any desire I may have had to return home to my family was denied.

To say that I was sick with grief, anger and even fear would be an understatement. Despite that, I was determined to keep my feelings hidden and under control, because having them known would not change a single thing. If anything, it could make things worse. Therefore, any crying or other demonstrations of discontent I felt rising to the surface, I reserved for the late hours of night, when I could use my pillow to quash them.

I was not in King Edward's care for very long before he dispatched me to the charge of Richard Neville, the Earl of Warwick. Warwick's northern stronghold at Middleham Castle served as my home and training ground for a number of years. It was there where I made the acquaintance of the king's youngest brother Richard Plantagenet, the Duke of

Gloucester. Our brief time together formed a bond of friendship that would be tested time and again. But it would ultimately prevail and evolve into a brotherhood that would transcend death.

I arrived at Middleham in the late afternoon of an abnormally cool summer's day. I wondered as my party approached, if the unusual temperature was indicative of the greeting I would receive. Feeling quite weary from my travels, I was not overly concerned. All I wanted was to stretch my legs and find a comfortable place to lay my head for a while.

I spent the last leg of my journey riding in a cart. My escorts believed that doing so would be a welcome relief after riding an exceedingly long time atop a horse. But I felt no better than a sack of grain in the sparsely cushioned wagon, which jostled me with every bump and turn in the road. My teeth slammed together so many times, they throbbed with pain. By the time I reached my destination, my jaw ached, my arse was numb, and my arms and legs were bruised from their repeated contact with the sides of the cart.

Just as my companions were about to retrieve me, I heard a loud and cheery "Hello!" coming from a short distance away.

I looked up to see a boy waving vigorously in the air while hurrying towards me. By the time my feet touched the ground, the lad was standing in front of me.

The boy was clearly a few years older than I, but surprisingly no less scrawny. I found it rather odd and slightly unnerving that he did not say anything at first, but simply stared at me with the most piercing of blue eyes. It seemed as though he was assessing me for some reason. I chose to stare back at him to show him I was not the slightest bit intimidated, even if I was.

"Welcome to Middleham Francis" he eventually announced rather loudly with the biggest of grins on his face. "I am Richard. You and I will be the best of friends. Come let us get you some refreshment," he said as he grabbed my hand and tugged me to move with him. "Someone will attend to your things."

That was Richard. Richard knew I would be scared after losing my father, as well as my home. He knew, because he felt the same way when his own father died and he had to leave the home he knew, to go to a place that was deemed more preferable by others. The only thing that made his situation more tolerable was the fact that he had some of his family with him. I, on the other hand, had no one.

To be alone in an unfamiliar place full of strangers was difficult. Richard understood this and more importantly felt compelled to make my transition easier. He knew when I was expected to arrive and made sure that his schedule would be free so that he would be available to greet me properly.

After making sure that my belly was full and my thirst was quenched, Richard gave me a tour of sorts. He showed me where I would be living and training, and then introduced me to many of the lads who I would be seeing on a regular basis. To my supreme disappointment and even confusion, they greeted me with the same level of enthusiasm one would have when cleaning a privy.

Richard told me not to take their frosty welcome personally. He explained that they were probably just tired and maybe even hungry. He then assured me that these boys were normally a reasonably likable bunch. I did not find his words reassuring in the least, and worried about how tired and unpleasant I would become in the near future.

Before returning to my quarters, which I will tell you about later, I made the acquaintance of some of the servants who would be tending to my needs during my stay. Richard was especially keen to point out that I was his friend, and as such, he expected them to treat me well. Most of them seemed preoccupied and not overly happy that there was someone else to deal with and take care of. I honestly could not blame them. It all seemed overwhelming. Although I had not yet begun the work that was expected of me, I knew I was in over my head.

As knights in training, we received instruction in a variety of intellectual, physical and social disciplines that occupied a great deal of our days and evenings. Our primary focus was with the use of arms, because we were expected above all things to be capable of defending our kingdom. It was perhaps a wise endeavor, given the volatility of the times we lived in.

Lacking the brawn and size of others, Richard and I realized early on that speed, wits and a good deal of luck would be our only chance in surviving any future confrontation.

I can remember us lying spent and bruised, leaning up against a pile of straw laughing like lunatics about our scrawny and battered bodies. What a pair we were. Needless to say, we both committed to spending countless hours honing our skills. We hoped our efforts would allow us to live to a ripe old age or at the very minimum until we bedded a few maidens. Thankfully, we at least lived long enough to fulfill the latter.

Although Richard studied strategy after strategy and practiced with every imaginable weapon, he found his greatest strength in the saddle. Not only was he a superb rider, but for some inexplicable reason, he was far more effective at besting opponents from atop a horse than from the ground. Oddly enough, sitting in a saddle allowed him to sustain greater endurance and wield weapons with greater force than when he was standing on two feet. I, on the other hand, could certainly hold my own on the back of a horse, but much preferred to face adversaries on steady ground in a battle.

While Richard favored a mace, I eventually became quite adept with a sword. Although I did not have weight in my favor, I was quick. I prayed that it would be enough should a challenge come my way. I think in retrospect that it has served me well. I know it also helped that my body eventually filled out and grew stronger and more muscular as time went on. Thanks be to God.

Training at Middleham was arduous and occupied long hours of the day. Sometimes I would be so tired I could barely move or keep my eyes open. I honestly do not know how I got through it. At least when Richard was around, I had someone to commiserate with. Unfortunately, most of my training would occur without him.

Richard, being older than I was, had already completed a good deal of his training before we met. Hence, he was destined to leave Middleham a lot sooner than he or I would have preferred.

His departure occurred just short of a year after my arrival. He tried to prolong his stay as much as he could. Unfortunately, having a king for a brother who had expectations and a hefty list of tasks requiring attention only made Richard's leaving more urgent. Thankfully, my friend was able to visit and send letters every now and then, despite having to travel a fairly long distance away. Almost two years after his departure from Middleham, Richard surprised us and was actually able to stay for a few months.

I know it may seem improbable for two people to become close friends in such a short time, but that is precisely what happened. Although Richard's brother was the king, he never treated me as someone who was inferior to him. He also never allowed his position to prevent him from spending time with me. Even our age difference did not seem to hinder our friendship. While we did not agree on everything, I never felt there was anything we could not say to one another.

We talked often about a great many topics. Richard especially loved to bring history into our conversations, because he thought there was much to be learned from the past. He found it particularly stimulating to conjecture about why people did what they did or how things might have worked out if they had done something different. Richard loved examining the strategies and motivations of historical figures. He also found it especially invigorating to babble on about the legendary King Arthur and his precious Camelot.

Richard truly admired Arthur's vision for the world and longed for someone to bring it into reality. To Richard's supreme annoyance, I would repeatedly remind him that things did not end well in Arthur's time regardless of his good intentions. I further asserted that there is no definitive evidence that the stories we have heard were nothing more than fanciful fabrications. Richard would practically scold me about how never trying was far worse than failure. He would then argue that just because we lack a means to prove that something is true, it in no way means that something is untrue.

I of course agreed, but never gave him the satisfaction in knowing it because I loved ruffling his feathers. Then to further plead his case, Richard would offer up the Almighty God himself, as an example of something many people believe exists even if there is no proof. And that, my dear diary, ended any further discussion on the matter, because there was absolutely no point in arguing with him about God or religion. The man was well versed and unbending on the subject. In fact, I truly believe that Richard would have made a fine priest had he been able to do without the more carnal pleasures of life.

I expect you may be thinking that it is rather peculiar that two young boys could have discussed such things or have that much to say about anything for that matter. Yet we did. I am not sure who had more opinions about the state of things since both of us seemed to relish analyzing and commenting upon virtually everything.

Unsurprisingly, our need to discuss and analyze things at length never changed. In fact, the older we were, the longer and more complicated our discussions became.

One could probably assume that our excessive need to blabber on stemmed from pure intellectual curiosity or having over expressive personalities. Looking back, however, I realize we were just trying to find some degree of understanding and comfort in a world where we lacked control over the state of our lives.

Richard's departure from Middleham was a perfect example of how little control we had. It served as a reminder that no matter how much I wanted things to stay the same, they would always change. And if I wanted to make it easy on myself, I knew I would have to be strong and flexible. I also knew I had to refrain from focusing too heavily on the things that were outside of my influence or control.

While I certainly missed having someone to talk to in such an in-depth way when Richard left, I kept myself fairly entertained in his absence. Although I never loved Middleham as Richard had, I do have some fond memories of the time I spent there, even though much of it was difficult.

I actually feel almost thankful for the challenges I experienced back then, because they taught me that I was much stronger than I thought. I just wish the years that followed had not tested me further.

3

IT'S ALL A GAME

As a child, many would describe me as being shy and having very little to say. In truth, I was neither shy nor lacking something to say or a means to say it. I was simply careful about where, what and when I chose to express or share, as well as with whom. My caution stemmed from having very little trust in anyone or anything.

People were rarely what they seemed and often took advantage of others for their own benefit. Bad things would regularly happen to good people. Disappointment and deception were commonplace and kindness was all too rare. What people did versus what they said they would do often differed greatly. Because of these very reasons, I was resolved to trust no one.

Although I may sound like one, surprisingly, my lack of trust did not make me a cynic. I actually believed that people were essentially good, even if they did not act that way all the time. Despite the many disheartening occurrences along the way, I also had faith that things could and would eventually get better. But it was clear to me however, even as a small boy, that life was a game of sorts. If I were to survive it and perhaps win it, I realized I would have to be careful and play it as smart as I could.

One might think having come from a privileged background I would not need to be concerned about such things. Although it did give me some advantages, my family's wealth and social standing never ensured my survival. In fact, sometimes, it put me at greater risk than someone with limited means and status. I knew I would have to use every ounce of courage and cleverness I had to avert danger and an untimely demise.

To facilitate safety and even victory in such a world, I recognized that staying out of trouble and avoiding the notice of others would be the best measure I could take. When someone stands out in some way, they become more vulnerable. They have more potential to be taken advantage of, be made an example of, or be required to do something they do not want to do. In the worst case, they may even be harmed or killed.

After my father died and I was subject to the whims of strangers, I became especially vigilant in my efforts to become absolutely invisible. I can say with utter certainty that having such a strategy served me well.

One of the most valuable skills I developed early on, aside from not being seen, was that of observation. By observing others words and actions, I could determine patterns and predict future behavior and responses. Doing so, presented me with many beneficial opportunities, but more importantly, it helped ensure my protection.

I admit that at times, I used the information I discerned from watching and listening to people to manipulate others in some way. However, I did not do this with any mal intent or egotistical motivations. My objective was simply to find some comfort in an uncomfortable situation and ultimately survive.

I know this may seem to be an odd and complicated thought process for a mere boy, but as you can tell, I did not think like other boys. In fact, during most of my childhood, I felt like an old man trapped in a young person's body.

I worried far more than others my age and obsessed for long hours at a time over options and strategies. I did this all in an attempt to stay a step ahead of others who could jeopardize my life or the world I lived in.

While I believe no child should have to think or behave this way, the harsh reality of our times made it difficult for me not to feel as I did. To illustrate my point, most memories of my father involve him preparing to go off to fight some battle or dealing with the aftermath of his return. I do not mean to imply that there were no lighthearted moments to reminisce over. It is just that carefree and happy times were all too infrequent. Hence, difficult times dear reader.

Needless to say, when I arrived at Middleham, I was as quiet and inconspicuous as I could possibly be. My attention was on full alert and I was determined to get through this ordeal as best as I could. I committed all of my energies to staying unnoticed and watching everything and everyone.

Richard, a keen observer in his own right, also lacked trust and believed that watching was one of the safest things one could do. Having this perspective in common made it easy for him to quickly recognize what I was doing. He had been at the game much longer than I and had become quite adept at making it work in his favor. And while he was eager to teach me what he knew, he was equally interested in hearing about my own observations and experiences.

Richard saw our similarities as an opportunity, one that could benefit both of us greatly. As such, he doggedly committed himself to gaining my trust and convincing me to join forces with him. By sharing what we have learned and observed on our own and combining our efforts, he believed we could develop better strategies and experience better outcomes.

"Together" he said, "we can do much more."

And he was right. Although we had little trust in others, for some reason I cannot explain, other than a shared sense of vulnerability, we trusted each other. That trust enabled us to combine our individual strengths to support our common purpose of survival. We honed, expanded and perfected our knowledge and skills, and together, developed tactics that provided greater comfort and security in our lives.

I have no doubt that I would not be alive today had we not had the perceptiveness, cleverness and even daring to do what we did. This may sound overdramatic. But I assure you, the times we lived in were difficult at best for adults, but were even more perilous to innocent children. The abilities we had, enabled us to avoid great danger on a regular basis.

They were also vital in helping me to get to where I am today.

You must be thinking, dearest reader, this all sounds very interesting in theory, but how did this work in reality? How did we use observation and the avoidance of notice in our favor? And what benefits did we really experience? I shall endeavor to give you examples of some of the areas of our lives where these skills came in quite handy.

Our sleeping quarters at Middleham would be considered unfit for animals. Yet the powers that be thought it would be the perfect location for their young charges to rest their tired achy bodies after hours of grueling training each day.

There were no soft beds or cushions upon which to lie, nor were there sufficient blankets to keep us warm. There were no comforts or conveniences of any kind for that matter. Only hard, worn pallets with thin straw mattresses and meager coverings awaited Middleham's youth.

Eleven or more boys shared a space within a structure designated for housing weaponry and tools. It was cold most of the time and very difficult to get a comfortable night's sleep. The lads who slept there often suffered from colds and other maladies due to the harsh conditions. But no one in authority seemed to care.

I think it is important for you to realize that these boys were not peasants or servants. They came from families of great wealth and power. Yet these young nobles were treated no better than vermin. The horses in the stables had better care and accommodation than the privileged youth. This made absolutely no sense to me, yet this sort of thing was done all the time. Even though the other lads seemed resigned to accept the situation, Richard and I were not.

Thankfully, Richard had already made some progress with respect to finding and securing alternative sleeping accommodations even before I arrived. But once we joined forces, we developed even better strategies that allowed us to sleep in more hospitable environments much more often. Because the other boys paid little attention to us, I do not think they ever recognized when we were gone.

Where did we go and how did we manage to do what others could not? Our commitment to avoiding notice and observing others' schedules and behavior presented certain opportunities for us. It allowed us to slip away and make connections that would prove highly beneficial to virtually every aspect of our lives.

Our most valuable alliances were made with important women of the keep, especially the older ones who were generally lonely, disregarded and bored. The many caretakers of Middleham, including the kitchen staff, maids, stable hands and stonemasons also played a significant role in improving our quality of life. Sadly, these hardworking people were often minimized, ignored and taken advantage of on a regular basis. These good men and women, who many disregarded, actually became our greatest allies, teachers, companions and even friends.

Our carefully woven network truly cared for Richard's and my wellbeing. They not only committed themselves to looking out for us, they made our miserable lives more comfortable, safe and even joyful. As much as they had a positive impact on our lives, please rest assured they also benefited from letting us into their private world and even their hearts.

We listened to them and valued their knowledge and efforts. We fetched, moved and lifted things for them, and even helped them complete tasks required by their jobs. We gave them the kindness, respect and attention they desired and deserved, along with a good deal of amusement along the way. And they were appreciative.

This group of kind and wonderful individuals made us rest and pampered us when we coughed or sniffed or looked a little tired or pale. When we were truly under the weather or ill, they were so protective and caring it made me weep.

Because Richard and I were exceedingly scrawny, our volunteer caretakers worried that we were starving and felt compelled to feed us whenever they could. They were also free with treats and gifts to make us smile and add to our comfort. When one of us was in jeopardy, these dear sweet people did not hesitate to create distractions so we could escape unscathed and live another day. I will be forever grateful for their selflessness and care.

These men and women not only helped and supported us, they educated us about life and how things worked. They shared their knowledge of horses, food preparation and a wide variety of other things that went into running a household and keeping a castle safe. We learned what made a wall strong or weak, how gate mechanisms worked, and many other fascinating and helpful things over the years. Unsurprisingly, much of this information would prove even more valuable when we were older and had more responsibility and dangers to deal with.

One of the most valuable things we learned back then was the importance of knowing what the powers that be were thinking or doing.

Those who run in the highest circles of society or have some authority frequently discuss highly sensitive and important matters in front of the many individuals who serve them. The people who do everything for them are disregarded like furniture pieces in a room. But they are not tables, chairs or any other object. They are flesh and blood human beings with minds and feelings, eyes and ears. They see and hear it all and cleverly take note of it.

Therefore, dear reader, if you wanted to know what was truly going on or what the master was thinking or worried about, you need only ask. Not just anyone though. Those who clean, serve food and drink, or tend to the horses are among the best sources of information. They know everything. Because these overworked, undervalued human beings were our friends, we knew everything too.

Knowing things was very helpful. Sadly, though, this sort of information did not always prevent us from being negatively impacted. Even so, Richard and I chose to count our victories when we had them. Happily, there were many of them.

While those in service proved to be exceptionally helpful to Richard and myself, the ladies of the keep also provided us with many benefits. These women, especially the older ones, were relegated to spend hours of each day in comfortable and beautifully decorated rooms with nothing to do. Well, at least nothing they really wanted to do. Men frequently ignored them and let them fend for themselves.

These delicately raised females were lonely, bored and desperate to be noticed and valued. Richard and I gave them what they truly wanted, something to look forward to. All of us were much happier for it.

The women received attention, kindness, compassion and amusement. In return, we gained a safe and comfortable place to spend some of our hours and a good deal of positive attention and entertainment as well. We also made sure that we never wore out our welcome by being as useful as we could. It also helped that we were cleaner than most of the other boys who roamed about Middleham and that these ladies were truly enamored by our cleverness and wit.

One of the biggest joys Richard had was being able to spend time reading. Books were precious to him, more so than normal riches that others typically valued. Because of this love, he amassed a truly impressive library over the years that any scholar or historian would envy. Unfortunately, the normal demands of life at Middleham for a young man, even the king's brother, gave little opportunity and time to pursue more pleasurable interests. That is, until we figured out how to avoid doing things we did not want to do and made the acquaintance of our devoted ladies.

Richard would frequently offer to read to the women. Eager for some fabulous tale that would bring excitement, adventure and even knowledge to their dull daily existence, they would always say yes. They listened with rapt attention and frequently made him read longer than he had intended. More often than not, they even felt compelled to clap when he was finished.

Richard delighted in the attention he received, as well as the comfortable surroundings and appetizing refreshments of which we both could partake. But my dear reader, the best thing about it, was that he could satisfy his own love of reading. I can still see the look on his face when they begged him to read more. It was all I could do not to laugh out loud.

You may probably be wondering what I was doing when Richard was giving his most masterful oratory performances. Please rest assured that I was not sitting idly just enjoying the spectacle, which was quite enjoyable I might add. I was committed to making myself as useful as he was. I just did it differently.

I poured refreshments, plumped up cushions, propped up feet, and frequently moved and fetched items for the ladies as they needed. To add to the amusement of a story or intensity of a moment, I offered commentaries and made sounds, which corresponded with the scene Richard was describing.

The ladies typically found my remarks to be insightful or humorous. They seemed particularly impressed with my imitation of creaking doors, howling winds and shrieking ladies. Richard thought they were unnecessary distractions and felt his dramatic recitation was sufficient to produce the ideal effect. The fact that I would do these things a lot longer than the scene warranted just plain annoyed him.

Sometimes, Richard would get so agitated he looked like he might jump up from his seat and hit me. But instead, he would just stop reading and sort of hold his breath and look like he was internally counting to ten. After what I am sure was only a few moments of silence, even though it seemed longer, he would exhale very slowly. Then in a calm and patient voice, like one would use with a child, he would say something like "alright Francis, I think everyone here knows there is a storm. I do not think we need to labor the point. So if I may continue without you howling in my ear, I would be ever so grateful."

Honestly, it took everything I had in me not to laugh while I murmured, "I am sorry. Please continue."

Despite my need to bring lightheartedness and humor to the situation, I took my time in these women's company seriously. I made their feelings a priority, listened intently and responded reassuringly to everything they said. I also frequently made admiring comments about their hairstyles, dresses and yarn creations, and even spent time untangling and spooling yarn. I wanted them to feel important and cared for as much as I wanted them entertained.

To add to our ladies' amusement and validation, on rare occasions, when the mood struck me, I would recite some poetic creation I made up spontaneously in the moment. They responded with glowing smiles and happy sighs, which was all the reward I needed. These women loved everything I did for them. They loved both of us, and devoted themselves to making us as happy and comfortable as we made them.

The hours spent with our female caretakers provided me with yet another benefit that I would not truly appreciate until I was older. They helped me to better understand how women thought and felt. This knowledge ultimately aided me in developing exceptional wooing skills that would later serve my more carnal needs quite well.

As you can tell, avoiding notice afforded us the time and ability to relax, rest, learn new things and even have a laugh. But as I have indicated before, it was also essential to getting out of doing things we had no desire to do. There always seemed to be a never ending list of dreary, thankless, and even dangerous tasks and responsibilities thrust upon the already burdened youth of Middleham. Richard and I were determined to do as little of it as possible.

We were not lazy by any means and worked hard every day. We were just clever enough to escape the unreasonable volume of tasks required, along with a few of the more heinous duties others would have us do.

We found that the best ways to escape notice and undesired duties was to hang back and stay in the middle of a group and never speak first or volunteer for anything. It was also a good idea not to be the first or last person to run away when one was given the freedom to do so. Being in the right place at the right time was another thing we tried very hard to accomplish. The fact that most people are fairly predictable helped with this endeavor.

One of the most useful things Richard and I could do to avoid being delegated unpleasant tasks and responsibilities was to deliver messages. I know what you are thinking. I just told you it was vital to never volunteer for anything. This, my dear reader, was a critical exception to the rule.

While most of the lads at Middleham considered such a task to be too boring and unimportant, Richard and I quickly recognized it for its amazing value. It provided a means for us to move about freely without scrutiny or difficulty. Of course, we had to run a lot, but it was worth it.

We frequently used the transporting of communications as an excuse to get out of doing something we did not like or to be anywhere else than where we were at the moment. All we needed to do was to emphasize that we had an important message to deliver and could not be delayed. This tactic worked beautifully every time.

As I have mentioned before, part of our days at Middleham required us to become adept at defending our kingdom from enemies and hopefully avoid dying in the process. Training for battle could be quite overwhelming and even hazardous especially when having to face opponents who are much bigger, stronger and aggressive than we were.

Having to develop fighting skills and gain comfort with a variety of weaponry was inevitable. We just wanted to do it on our own terms, so that we could avoid major damage to our bodies and again, maybe live to bed a few maidens.

Boys and men are typically competitive and driven to prove that they are stronger and tougher than those around them. Therefore, the potential for injury or worse was high even under the best of circumstances. While some of the lads we could face in training gave us concern, the person who taught fighting skills and coordinated training was far more terrifying.

The master of arms was especially fond of encouraging older and much bigger lads to beat up on younger and smaller boys. This despicable man claimed that it was for our own good. "You will thank me later," he would often say, as he snickered and muttered a string of demeaning names like "milksops" under his breath.

He defended his actions, reasoning that it would make us tough enough to survive whatever life may thrust upon us in the future. I personally think he just enjoyed brutality and chipping away at people's confidence and sense of power. Because he was cruel and took pleasure in others' discomfort, Richard and I made it our mission to avoid the man at all costs. Thankfully, it became less necessary to interact with him as time went on.

Returning to the topic of our sleeping arrangements, Richard and I often felt like nomads. We were constantly on the move, searching for that safe and comfortable place to sleep. Less traveled alcoves or unoccupied rooms in the castle served as our temporary quarters many a night. Although they typically lacked a fire, we made due with what we had. With a few cushions and blankets we found scattered around the keep, we could create a perfect makeshift bed upon which we could get a reasonable night's rest.

But our preferred and most comfortable place to sleep by far was in one of the ladies' sitting rooms, usually at their insistence. All of their rooms were abundant with cushions and knitted blankets, food and drink. They were also always warm from continuously stoked fires.

The ladies welcomed us to their private spaces like long lost family. They were especially persistent about us staying with them when we were sick or looking paler than usual, which according to their opinion was far too often.

I will have to admit, Richard and I took advantage of the ladies' caring natures by sometimes pretending to be unwell if we were especially weary, cold or desperate. Not wanting something bad to happen to us, they chose to err on the side of spoiling us, rather than leaving things to chance. And we were grateful.

Another popular spot used for sleeping, not only by Richard and myself, but by others as well, was the great hall in front of the huge fireplace that stood in its center. On especially cold evenings, even the lords of Middleham encouraged people to take warmth where they could. Although I cannot prove it, I suspect others like Richard and myself were seeking out better sleeping accommodations more frequently than the lord of the keep would expect or approve of. And who could blame them?

4

KEEPING ONE'S HUMOR IS IMPORTANT

As I have alluded to, despite what others might think, living in these times was often difficult even if you had title or resources. Because the future was terribly unpredictable, it was easy to lose one's cheeriness and even hope. For these reasons, Richard and I tried to find humor wherever we could.

Despite the uncertainties of life, we chose to live in the moment and have as much fun while it lasted. Richard and I were not troublemakers or ruffians by any means. But we did bend the rules a bit every now and then. In retrospect, I probably bent them a little more than he did.

Neither one of us could have predicted what lie ahead in our future. Perhaps that is a good thing. I would not have wanted to waste a single moment worrying before we needed to. That is, unless doing so, could have resulted in a more favorable outcome for all of us.

I would like to think I was the comical relief to the unfortunate reality of our lives. While I found amusement in the everyday things, it became a challenge of sorts for me to bring levity to Richard. If you were to ask him, I am sure he would say that my romantic escapades and poetic creations brought him the most entertainment throughout the years of our acquaintance.

I remember one incident in particular that left us both in hysterics. I was still in my early years of wooing and eager to test my skills with the ladies should an opportunity present itself.

Richard and I were riding along a country road on our way to some appointment when we came upon a golden haired maiden of considerable beauty and naivety. I greeted the girl with one of my famous smiles, and then proceeded to charm her with an abundance of flowery words and longing glances. I did not have to turn around to know that Richard was rolling his eyes and choking to suppress his laughter.

Feeling quite confident with myself, I professed to have deep feelings for the maiden that I have carried since seeing her at an earlier date. I explained that I had written a poem in hopes that when I saw her again she would know of my love for her.

The girl looked both happy and puzzled by my declaration. "Do you mean to say dear sir, it is me, Alice, of whom you speak?" she hesitantly asked gazing hopefully into my eyes. "Perhaps you have confused me with someone else?"

"No," I said with my hand over my heart, "There is no mistake. It is you of whom I speak. It is Alice of whom I dream. You are indeed the muse for my poetic creation."

Finally satisfied, sweet Alice then informed me that she was ready to hear what I had written. The girl practically held her breath as she waited for me to retrieve my romantic declarations from the leather satchel I carried behind me.

It took a full minute before I found what I was looking for. "Ah, here it is," I said, grasping the paper tightly in my fist, as I flashed her another grin.

She fixed her gaze on my hand as her lips curved into a smile that was truly intoxicating. I could almost imagine her heart speeding up in anticipation. In my head, I made a silent prayer that neither of us would be disappointed. I unfolded the blank piece of parchment and slowly scanned the page as if I were actually reading something. Yes, dear diary, I was attempting to create an illusion. I then proceeded to recite the most passionate verses in perfect rhyme at the top of my head.

The girl was so overtaken with emotion I thought she might swoon. Victory was at my grasp, I thought, as I internally rejoiced at the carnal pleasure that would soon be mine. Richard, feeling both nauseous and mischievous at that moment, decided to punish me for my arrogance.

"Oh Francis, that was beautiful" he said, clapping a little too loudly and wildly for my taste. "You are a true master of the written word, an artist. You must read it again."

The girl's head bobbed up and down in agreement while her wide innocent blue eyes stared adoringly at me. "Yes, please" was all she said, as my stomach started to ache.

Knowing full well that I could not do as she asked, Richard flashed his best smile and nodded vigorously as he seconded her plea with his own.

Murder was not an option, nor was an exact reciting of the poetic masterpiece I created spontaneously just a few minutes before. Richard seemed to relish in my momentary squirming and dilemma and had to fight hard not to laugh out loud. I was not amused.

I eventually made some excuse about not wanting to minimize my words by having to repeat them, and then apologized for having to leave for an important meeting. I bid the starry eyed maiden farewell and rode off with Richard and the men who accompanied us, howling in my wake.

We referred to the event in question many times over the years in an effort to lighten up the moment at hand. It would forever be known to us as "Almost Alice with the Chalice." Obviously, "Almost" is a reminder of how close I came to winning the maiden's favor. The other words reference part of my spontaneous poetic invention. I could not have come up with two words that rhymed more perfectly together. Sadly, they were also the only part of my poem that I could ever recall. At the mere mention of "Almost Alice with the Chalice," we could not hold back our laughter. It was by far one of the funniest memories we had.

Humor was an essential element of our survival in a world that was not always inclined to support what we believed and desired. All too frequently, the thoughts and behaviors of people around us differed greatly from what Richard and I chose to think and act upon. Had we not found some means to bring forth some amusing distraction, our frustration and sadness about this disparity could have quickly escalated to hopelessness.

The views and behavior of the Tudors in particular were the complete opposite of everything we thought and hoped for, and thus caused us the greatest offense. They offered neither peace nor fairness. In a world that needed more light, they fostered even greater darkness.

The Tudors had no honor and were nothing more than bullies who employed manipulation and brute force rather than a demonstration of true leadership to gain favor and power. They discarded, ruined, or if need be, killed anyone who would get in their way. Richard was one of those individuals who they set out to destroy for their own personal gain.

They tarnished his reputation and ultimately took his life. No matter what lies the Tudors continue to propagate, both the Lord Almighty and I know the truth and a few other secrets that they would kill to know.

The Tudors frequently underestimated the courage and intellect of others. Contrary to what they would have you believe, Richard was one of the most honorable and intelligent persons I have known. Despite that, he did not always have the answer. None of us did. Sometimes there was no answer, or at least one we liked.

Unfortunately, sometimes the choice came down to doing something or doing nothing at all. Many times, it did not matter what you did or which way you turned, because disaster was waiting at every end. You just hoped you took the path that was the lesser of the evils.

Although Richard never liked having to make decisions, he had a responsibility to make them. He wore a crown. With it came the not so pleasant task of deciding something in hopes that it may come to some good end. The problem was that there were endless decisions to make and they did not always yield the desired outcome. And it would seem, every choice that had to be made, became more difficult as time went on. Wanting to make the best ones he could, Richard sought advice from me and others he trusted. He hoped that between all of us, we would somehow have the ability to know the best course of action for each situation.

Every so often, with little to no information available to help in our decision making, the only option was to guess. Sadly, there were no guarantees that things would have turned out as we wanted, even if extensive intelligence was at our disposal and Richard's choice was well thought out. Sometimes there were just too many variables for things to work in our favor. Unsurprisingly, when something does not end up the way someone wants despite his or her best efforts, it is easy to get disheartened.

Richard believed at his core that no matter how disappointed or despaired one may become, they should never give in to discouragement or stop trying. His mother Cecily drilled this concept into him for most of his life. She lived by a rule that was passed down from generation to generation in her family. As others who came before her, she was determined to ensure that all of her children lived by it too.

Cecily was as strong as she was difficult. There was nothing soft or smooth, cozy or warm about her. This woman was a survivor and as tough as anyone I have ever met. As such, no one wanted to be on her bad side. She was reluctant to compromise and willing to do anything in order to get her way.

She thought she was clever and restrained in her manipulations of others, but there was nothing subtle about her. Life unfortunately, did not help. Cecily endured many losses, obstacles and tragedies over the years. Most people would not have been able to bear even a small fraction of what she suffered. But Cecily never gave up or behaved as though she was any less because of it.

She repeatedly insisted that the only thing that enabled her to get through it all was her bloody rule. It also made her family the way they were and helped them accomplish much of what they achieved.

Her rule was simply, "No matter what the situation, never step down or to the side. Always step up, rise over and become more powerful."

This type of thinking relies on a person's ability to will themselves to push through, even in the darkest of moments. It also does not leave a lot of flexibility or options for someone.

While I myself chose not to let things go after Richard died, I did not stay and fight out of some desire to prove that I was not weak. Nor did I feel some twisted need to endure as Cecily had endured, despite wishing to survive. While at times I had to force myself to get out of bed and try again, I cannot even imagine doing that day in and day out year after year. Moreover, let me be very clear, I have never desired power or any of the burdens that go with it. I stayed because I wanted to.

Cecily was not the only one who thought the way she did. In fact, given the volatility of the times we lived in, there was a constant and unspoken pressure for people to be always at their best. One could not beg off even if they were weary, under the weather or dealing with some tragedy of sorts. If your body was still somewhat intact and you still had your senses, you were expected to carry on. However, doing so was not always easy.

The challenges and dangers of our world could make anyone feel scared or overwhelmed on a regular basis. Not everyone was strong or capable of keeping his or her footing in such circumstances. But Richard and I were careful, cautious and even vigilant, and rarely gave in to fear. It was not something we could afford.

Anger was another thing we felt was important to keep in check to some degree. We knew if we let it get out of control, we could do something stupid, and it could become perilous to our health and maybe even get us killed. We also recognized how succumbing to the grief and loss of loved ones and friends was a useless endeavor if we were to survive.

Richard and I also accepted the fact that we were still human. We knew that holding in our feelings all the time was not prudent if we were to remain reasonably sane and comfortable. To this end, we periodically allowed ourselves brief moments of wallowing and other negative emotional demonstrations, hoping it would help us stay calm and relatively stable. As I have already indicated, we also chose to keep our heads by employing humor wherever we could. We came to the conclusion early on that it was far better to laugh than to cry.

But sometimes it was difficult to smile, let alone say or do funny things when life was anything but mirth inspiring. Since Richard's death, I have found it near impossible to keep my chin up and find humor and even hope. Now, dear reader, that I have all this time on my hands to ponder that which has transpired, I find myself engaging in wallowing far too often. Even the thought of "Almost Alice with the Chalice," does not produce the usual response. I fear I will have no humor when this is all said and done.

5

A QUESTION OF LOYALTY

Civil war has plagued this country for as long as I can remember. The conflict, of which I speak, has waged between the house of Lancaster and the house of York, two rival branches of the house of Plantagenet[3]. These adversaries having been fighting for the throne of England on and off over a span of nearly three decades. To my recollection, the crown has changed hands at least five times during this period of upheaval.

Each side in this dispute held a distinctly different opinion as to what constituted a legitimate royal

---

[3] Historians commonly refer to this conflict as the War of the Roses, due to the rose emblems associated with each house. The Yorkists were represented by a white rose and the Lancastrians by a red one. When King Henry VII took the crown and married Richard III's niece Elizabeth of York, he theoretically united both houses. To allegedly promote further unity he adopted a new Tudor rose emblem that incorporated both red and white.

claim. While there were true loyalists on either side, people frequently switched sides in hopes of retaining their heads and land, and keeping their coffers full.

The crown was most recently taken by the Lancastrian Henry Tudor when he defeated my friend and liege, the Yorkist King Richard III. While there were subsequent challenges to his throne, it is to my deep despair that loathsome Henry still rules this land.

It is probably important to mention that my family had long been supporters of the house of Lancaster. I eventually chose to break with tradition and pledge my allegiance to the Yorkist cause and more specifically Richard.

It all began when the Yorkists took victory over the Lancastrians and Edward became king. Naturally, I was expected to support and be loyal to our new sovereign even though my father had fought for his rival. As a child, there really was no choice in the matter. Unsurprisingly, my options would be further constrained when Edward took me as his ward and made Warwick my guardian.

As you know, Richard quickly became one of a select few whom I trusted and respected. Because he was loyal to his brother, it made it easier for me to be loyal to his brother.

Sadly, while I was still under Warwick's guardianship, Warwick rebelled against Edward with the intention of taking away his crown. Had Warwick been successful, his plan was to replace Edward with Edward's brother George. Despite my lack of participation in Warwick's actions against Edward, my loyalty would nevertheless be in question. I was essentially guilty by association.

After Warwick was defeated and killed, Edward granted me a pardon with the condition that I swear my allegiance to him. Since I was underage and had no resources, financial or otherwise at my disposal, and also wanted to live, I had no alternative or say in the matter.

In truth, at that point, I really did not have to be overly concerned for my life. My supposed loyalty to Warwick was not by choice, nor did I personally betray Edward. Had I been older or foolish enough to take up arms against Edward, choice or not, it may have cost me my life. Thankfully, that was not the case.

Regardless, I had already committed my fealty to Edward prior to this whole ordeal and saw no difficultly in maintaining it. Then obviously, once

Richard became king, I easily pledged my support and loyalty to him.

Although, my becoming a Yorkist was not my choice in the beginning, it eventually became my choice. And I have not regretted my decision to align myself with their cause, even though the other side eventually won.

Despite his general lack of trust in others, Richard truly valued and expected loyalty. He placed so much importance on the virtue, he made it part of his motto, "Loyalty Binds Me." Richard gave it and desired it from others. Sadly and unsurprisingly, he did not always receive it. In the end, his inability to get it, let alone keep it, ultimately cost him his life.

Betrayal is a bitter pill to swallow for anyone, but for Richard it was much worse. It tore at his very soul. Some would have called him a bloody fool for giving people the opportunity to disappoint and betray him time and again. I myself have accused him on more than one occasion of being one, but in reality, Richard was no fool. He just had his own stubborn, principled and perhaps naive view of the world.

Richard lived by a code that he was reluctant to change. While the principles to which he based them upon were noble, they were not always realistic or safe.

Among many things, Richard believed that given enough chances, people will eventually do the right thing. I knew that however dispiriting it might be, some individuals are simply not capable, and some would not even want to be. And if one's betrayer is someone they once called friend or with whom they fought alongside, the reality of their treachery can be more than one can bear.

When I think about the people who turned against Richard and contributed to his death, I am struck with overwhelming anger and grief. The only thing that gives me comfort is my belief that one day they will pay for what they have done.

Betrayal is bad enough when it occurs among acquaintances and friends, but when it is upon family it is heinous indeed. Richard viewed family to be the most important thing, after the Lord Almighty, of course. In fact, when it came to family, he would make the supreme exception by ignoring all his rules about not trusting anyone, even if it killed him.

Unfortunately, blood does not always dictate compatibility or loyalty. It is a hard lesson to accept that even a member of one's family can knowingly deceive or wish to cause them harm.

Sadly, Richard's code and tender heart would repeatedly blind him to the deceit and ill will of others in his midst, until it was too late. Despite that, he was reluctant to relinquish his hope and faith in others and thus, would be tested time and again.

Richard's jealous and greedy brother George challenged the patience, love, loyalty and trust of Edward too many times, and ultimately lost his life because of it. Richard could not accept the reality of who George really was.

Even when things were at their worst, Richard continued to cling to an unrealistic belief that George would eventually come to his senses and do what was right and honorable. Alas, poor Richard was doomed to be disappointed.

While I am not the kind of person who relishes the idea of lopping off people's heads, sometimes it comes down to a choice. It is either yours or theirs. Suffice it to say, Richard understood this reality even if he did not like it. Unfortunately, we did not always agree upon who or when.

I often wonder how things would have turned out had Richard taken off some of the heads I found particularly egregious or at minimum, sent them into exile. Margaret Beaufort, Henry's trouble making, lunatic of a mother, comes to mind as one of those people I would have handled differently. Had it been up to me, she would have spent the remaining years of her life in a dark and distant cave or a remote cloistered convent. But Richard would not hear of it.

I would like to think he is looking down at me from heaven as I write these words and is whispering in my ear, "you were right Francis."

Now when Richard did feel compelled to act, there was no stopping him. One time in particular, he made up his mind and responded so swiftly, I, myself was caught by surprise.

The event in question involved William Hastings, Lord Chamberlain[4] and Edward's longtime friend. Because Hastings had the unwavering trust of his brother, and he was well regarded by Richard himself,

---

[4] The Lord Chamberlain is the most senior officer of the royal household. His primary responsibility is to oversee those who support and provide advice to the king, and is an advisor in his own right sworn to the Privy Council. The Lord Chamberlain also participates in the planning and coordination of courtly functions and appointments, but more importantly is frequently called upon to act as the king's spokesman in council and parliament. His influence is so great, he has the power to facilitate or restrict communication and access to the king.

he continued on as Lord Chamberlain after Edward's death. Neither Richard nor I would have imagined anything untoward from the man, given his history. In truth, Hastings in many ways was like a member of the family, which made what transpired even more heartbreaking.

Both Richard and I agreed that it was a good idea to keep your enemies close and to never underestimate them or let your guard down even when all seemed quiet. There is often a calm before a storm. People typically regroup and make plans during those times and then attack when you least expect it. Trust should never be given unless it is earned. Even if it is earned, it should never be taken for granted. Life experience has taught us these things and we were determined never to forget them.

While we held hope that people were as they claimed to be, neither Richard or myself was willing to risk everything on hope alone. Presumably, the more information one had, the better the decisions they could make, and the less they would be caught off guard. Richard was determined to have the advantage and learned early on the importance of having carefully placed spies to gather information and thwart off treachery before it was too late.

When Richard learned of Hastings' treasonous deeds and plans, he was enraged. There was no consultation with his council, not even myself. An order was issued to find Hastings and bring him immediately to Richard's personal chambers to answer to the charge. Richard was not going to make the same mistake with Hastings that Edward made with his brother George. If the allegations were true, friend or no friend, second chances were no longer an option.

When Richard confronted the man, Hastings did not deny the accusations nor did he plead for his own life. Richard responded by calling for his immediate execution. Before Richard took Hastings' head, he assured him that his family would be taken care of. Richard also granted him certain exceptions that typically would not be given to a traitor. As promised, Hastings' wife and sons were allowed to inherit his lands and properties. He was also given an honorable burial despite his dishonorable behavior. His body was laid to rest in St. George's Chapel in Windsor next to his dear friend, King Edward IV.

I can only surmise that Richard was more decisive in this case because he held Hastings to a higher standard than most. Hastings was expected to do better, because he knew better. I think that is why he did not bother to try to explain himself. He violated the code and trust he pledged to uphold. There was nothing Hastings could say to defend that. Even so, it was probably one of the hardest decisions Richard had to make, even if it was the right one.

I had no knowledge of any of this until Hastings was dead. Shortly after the shocking deed was done, Richard requested my immediate presence. I arrived in haste with my gut churning in anticipation of what I might hear. I found Richard pacing and wringing his hands, looking as pale as the moon in a crisp night sky. I asked him what happened and he told me what I told you.

He never provided any details of the betrayal for which Hastings was put to death. Richard simply said it was too heinous to voice aloud. Even though he would be judged for his seemingly impulsive actions, he was determined to never let anyone else know why. He also felt strongly that no one, aside from himself, would be made vulnerable by what he did. That is why he never sought council from anyone including myself.

After Richard confessed what had transpired, he began to sob. He was not looking for any comfort or reassurance; he only wanted to cry. He cried like a baby for what seemed like an eternity. And when his tears seemed to finally dry up, he started to vomit. As I watched my poor friend retch like a man who had been poisoned, I could no longer hold back my own tears.

While I looked at the shadow of a man who was hunched before me, I thought about all those people out in the world who were convinced he was cold and heartless. They would never know what I know. Richard did have a heart. A big one. It was simply broken.

As I now sit staring at the sides of the rough wooden table I scribble away at day after day, I find myself thinking about how people are always choosing sides. The side of the law. The side in a tournament. The side in a battle. My side. Your side.

Sides are also never drawn without giving them some value. This is the good side. This is the bad side. The right side. The wrong side. It all depends on your perspective. Obviously, no one in their right mind would ever refer to their own side as being bad or wrong. You get my meaning.

Once a person commits to a particular side, they need to identify those who belong to the same side.

Should a conflict arise, this would ensure that they would fight against the right people.

Sometimes however, people may not be able to tell who is truly on their side or against them until it is too late. Sadly, an individual may pretend to be on one side, when in reality they are loyal to another. Even if someone can tell the good from the bad, they may still choose to give their support to the less desirable side, simply because they are afraid.

I cannot blame people for feeling scared. Everyone including myself has experienced the unpleasant emotion at one time or another. Unfortunately, fear can make the smartest people stupid, and what results from choices made out of fear can be even scarier. One should be careful not to let it skew their thinking too much or they could make decisions that they will come to regret. Or even worse, they could lose the very things they feared would be lost if they had not chosen the side they did.

I much prefer to honor my truth and die, than to sacrifice it in some vain attempt to keep on living. One could say Richard is not the only one who could be stubborn or principled.

6

KINGS, GOD AND MEN

Dearest diary, today I find myself pondering the role of God in the making of kings. Most people subscribe to the notion that beyond lineage, a king becomes a king out of some divine right. "It is God's will," many would say when the royal of their choice is granted victory over another contender for the throne. Richard himself believed this to be so.

I wonder, does God really choose sides? Does God delight in the death of some of his children so as to favor another of his children? And what does it say about this theory and God himself, when a crown can switch back and forth as the years go by?

Do people pray more or less for their side at different times? Is God fickle? Can he not make up his mind who is his favorite? Or dear reader, is the Lord Almighty sitting back and shaking his head at the supreme arrogance, greed, stupidity and stubbornness of his creations? Perhaps he is feeling a tad regretful about his gift of free will that many of my peers take full advantage of and abuse with great regularity.

As a reasonably religious man, I have tried my utmost to live in a way that adheres to a majority of biblical doctrine and hopefully cause little offense to whom I pray. But in all honesty, I have questioned and even doubted the validity of certain church tenets and teachings at various times in my life. I have also found myself challenging others' interpretations of what God is and what He is thinking and doing on a daily basis.

One of the things that I find myself questioning and disagreeing about involves God's alleged involvement in king making. Admittedly, I do believe in some degree of destiny. However, I do not believe that our creator is in the business of designating who will wear a crown or who shall live and die to make it all possible.

I will continue to pray for God's love, mercy, protection and support, and that which I perceive as right prevails. But I would be foolhardy to expect that He values my requests above all others.

My words on this matter are not meant to be disrespectful or blasphemous. They are simply intended to show how one's beliefs can figure greatly into justifying one's actions. And because these beliefs could be questionable, so could one's actions. It is just something to think about.

You may not know this, but men have two brains. One lives inside their head, while the other stays hidden in their breeches. The brain in one's head is usually considered the better of the two. Therefore, when the lower brain asserts dominance over the upper one, undesired consequences typically result.

What am I talking about? As brave and strong, and yes as smart as King Edward may have been, he unfortunately let his prick dictate too many of his decisions.

While there is no denying Edward did much good while he was king, his lower brain decisions would cost him and this country a great deal. To his credit, the kingdom enjoyed years of peace and greater prosperity under his rule. Unfortunately, he would jeopardize it all in order to satisfy his more carnal urgings.

Edward's wife and queen, Elizabeth Woodville is a beautiful and ambitious woman. She used her feminine wiles to coax him into doing her bidding and giving favor to her family over others who had been loyal and even responsible for his being king.

The Woodvilles were greedy, self promoting, power hungry, manipulative and willing to do whatever was necessary to get what they wanted. They were definitely not the best people to trust with authority or riches. The fact that they fought on the side of the Lancastrians prior to Edward becoming king did not seem to matter. He essentially gave them free rein to lay siege to this country. But the woman in his bed was happy, and thus Edward was happy.

One of the biggest mistakes Edward made, again at the urging of his bride, was to minimize and betray my former guardian after he helped Edward become king.

Naturally, Warwick was furious. The man also felt unappreciated, disregarded and more than uncertain about his future. Most of all, he was scared. These feelings grew into a desperation that would cause him to do the unthinkable and attempt to take the crown away from Edward. The plan he put into place was ripe with disaster.

The first mistake Warwick made was to align himself with Edward's jealous and backstabbing brother George who was hungry for the throne. He then forced his daughter Isabel into marrying George with the intention of her one day becoming queen.

Warwick's desperation also led him to go crawling to Margaret of Anjou in hopes of securing her help in his rebellion against Edward. This woman was responsible for the death of his father. As such, his greatest wish prior to this time was to see her dead. I have absolutely no idea how he could even bear to be in her presence, let alone the long hours I imagine they spent together making plans.

But having Margaret's assistance required him to forfeit more than his own pride and wishes. To seal the deal, he sacrificed his daughter Anne to his enemy's son in order to obtain the troops he needed. This was the very same Anne, I might add, who would later become Richard's wife.

Warwick made bargains with the devil everywhere he could, but the devil lost, as did Warwick. As for my former guardian, he was no longer alive for it to matter. While he was able to escape with death, his poor family suffered greatly for his choices.

I imagine Warwick felt totally justified in his actions despite how things turned out. I am certain he would point the blame entirely at Edward. In truth, I am not sure that I would disagree with him.

While it is hard to justify disloyalty, in all honesty, I cannot truly judge Warwick for going to the other side and fighting against Edward. Edward did not really leave him any choice. Unfortunately, by the time Edward realized his mistake, it was too late to make things right.

I know we cannot change that which has already passed, but I find myself playing this particular what if, over and over in my head nonetheless. I try not to linger on such things, but I cannot seem to help myself, because my heart still aches for what could have been.

Had Edward been less of a selfish idiot and acted more honorably, things would have been very different for all of us. Richard would not have needed to clean up such a big mess upon taking the crown. But more significantly, the kingdom would have been more unified and there would have been fewer reasons and less opportunity for Henry to come in and take it all away. Damn you Edward. And damn your lower brain.

7

THE BUSINESS OF LOVE

I always envied Richard for being able to marry someone he loved. Naturally, there were benefits to his marriage beyond his affections, such as becoming master of his beloved Middleham. But the fact that he could have these things with a woman he loved was a rare and wonderful gift.

You see my devoted reader, regardless of one's position or financial resources, love generally has little bearing on whether or not a person marries. To many, marriage is simply a means to an end, and sadly is often more about survival and security than anything else. Marriage could easily be the difference between keeping or losing one's home or land or becoming destitute or worse.

While both sexes may marry out of desperation, it is particularly an issue for women. The laws of our land subject women to many more restrictions than their male counterparts. This unfortunately limits their options and makes them quite vulnerable.

In reality, unless there is a male family member willing to provide for her needs, it may not leave a female with much choice. If she is unable to secure a job in service or is unwilling to spend her life cloistered in a convent, marriage may be a woman's only hope. Sadly, that hope may turn out to be more of a curse than a gift. The person she marries is rarely if ever her choice. And most of the time that choice will be down to the lesser of evils.

Unfortunately, even if someone does have a choice or has better resources available to them, they can still select to go against their true desire. More often than not, they will still make a marriage of convenience rather than succumbing to more romantic notions and wishes.

Matters of the heart are especially of little concern to the privileged and powerful. One's wealth, property, title, social standing and politics, along with the king's wishes, tend to play a more significant role in the making of matches than love. Wedded unions frequently feel more like business contracts rather than a joining of affections.

The lengths to which people will go in order to broker what is deemed a good marriage may appear extreme and even ludicrous. But for those who engage in such negotiations, this is viewed as a perfectly sound and necessary endeavor.

And while there is an occasion for these arranged couplings to grow into compatible, joyful or perhaps even loving unions, the majority will suffer unhappiness and often feel trapped.

Naturally, one could always take a mistress or lover who is far more suitable both in and out of bed. Many see this as their best option to fill the void or at the very least distract them from their daily woes. In fact, this practice has become so commonplace, it generally goes on without anyone ever noticing. It is the rare love match or case of fidelity that causes more raised eyebrows and gossip than romantic liaisons outside of a marriage.

I, like so many others, was robbed of any choice in the matter of selecting a bride. Shortly before celebrating my tenth birthday, I was married off to Warwick's niece Anne Fitzhugh, who was only five years old at the time. Anne was a sweet enough girl, but she was not someone I would have chosen for my wife, let alone at such a young age.

Our hasty union was simply a way for my guardian to obtain a firmer grasp upon my family's wealth and property, and a tighter rein over my life. I feel sick just thinking about it and the many years I had to fight for what was rightfully mine. I was also angry and tempted to use some of my newly gained warfare skills to teach the adults who were ruining my life a richly deserved lesson. But because I also liked my head comfortably attached to the top of my body, I refrained from any violent demonstration of my dissatisfaction.

Soon after our marriage vows were exchanged and the ink detailing the terms of our ridiculous union was dry, I returned to Middleham to continue my training. I spent the next three years with little thought of my marriage and what it could mean for my future. Then suddenly I was informed that I was being sent to live with my child bride and her family. I dreaded the thought of living among yet another group of strangers rather than my own family, but did what was expected of me anyway.

I will have to say though, to my surprise, Anne's family was kind and welcoming and made what could have been a difficult experience much easier. You should know before your imagination and even horror takes over, I did not live as man and wife with Anne until many years had passed. I waited until my bride was old enough and deemed she was ready to make our relationship more intimate before consummating our union.

While Anne and I eventually developed a degree of fondness for one another, sadly, it never evolved into anything more. I am sure the fact that I was frequently away from home on business of the king did not help. We did have a few things in common, however, our greatest impediment was our differences.

She was shy and had little to say most of the time, while I was more outgoing and perhaps talked too much. When we did speak, I would have greatly enjoyed engaging in deeper more complicated discussions, but she much preferred to keep our conversations about lighter more trivial topics.

In fairness though, women were generally discouraged from speaking with men let alone in some in-depth way. But unlike many of my peers, I valued the thoughts, ideas and opinions of women and always encouraged them to speak their mind freely. Regardless, Anne chose to express very little, and as such, I really did not know how she truly thought and felt about many things. It would seem that my wife felt perfectly comfortable about keeping it that way.

Anne was truly happiest when she was in quiet contemplation or prayer. I often think she would have had greater contentment in life as a nun.

Her uneasiness in conversing with others was not the only thing I found disconcerting. Anne also lacked any desire to know about things in our world. Although she could read and write, my wife had very little education and had no interest in expanding upon her knowledge. It was one of the things that bothered me most about her.

I was curious from the day I left my mother's womb. I loved learning new things. Everything was a wonderful mystery and puzzle for me to explore and solve. I could not understand why Anne would reject the opportunity to know more than just the simplest of things to get by.

Other husbands were far more controlling than I was. These men, who long suffered from fragile egos found it difficult to accept that their wives may be as smart if not smarter than they were. I never thought that way. But it did not matter. Anne had no desire to elevate herself or connect differently with others.

Also sadly and surprisingly, despite the volatility of the times we lived in, my wife seldom concerned herself with the goings on of things in the kingdom and rarely gave in to worry. I, on the other hand, was heavily aware of what was happening because of my involvement in the affairs of the king, and as such frequently succumbed to worry.

Anne's naivety and ignorance also made her particularly vulnerable in the company of others. Not only did it make her more prone to being taken advantage of or manipulated, it also made it more likely for her words or actions to put one or both of us at risk. For this reason, after Richard was defeated and killed, I chose to go into hiding and let her think that I was dead. I knew that if she believed that I was dead, others would believe that I was dead. While it may seem cruel, it really was safer for both of us.

Please understand, I do not believe that my wife would intentionally wish to do either of us any harm. On the contrary, I actually think Anne would want to be helpful, but would not have the slightest inclination of any danger in doing so. Her contacts were questionable at best. More importantly, she could inadvertently say or do something around the wrong person and cause my already precarious situation to get worse.

I cannot trust her to protect my secret. Therefore, dead I shall stay.

Aside from our many intellectual and communication differences, my wife's lack of interest in poetry, music and dancing was also a profound disappointment. I adored poetry and entertainments of all sorts, and would have attended every ball and musical performance to which I was invited had time permitted.

Despite having nothing in common, Anne and I rarely if ever argued. Given that our discussions were generally brief and superficial exchanges, it was fairly easy to keep things cordial. Although the time we spent in each other's company was tolerable if not occasionally pleasant, we both would have preferred to share our time with someone else.

I know my words may appear to be harsh, but they are not said with spite or malice. I have no ill will for my wife, nor would I want her to be hurt or unhappy. Although my marriage was not unbearable, it was not what either of us wanted. The simple truth is that we would have happily traded our amicable relationship for deeper connection and love, something that unfortunately we could not find with each other.

I confess that given the lack of connection and fulfillment in my marriage, I felt compelled to go outside of it in hopes of filling the void it left within my heart.

I suspect you think me a cad, but I was a lonely man with a desperate desire to love and be loved. That is not to say that the urgings of my lower brain did not yearn for more physical stimulation and pleasure, because they did. But my romantic liaisons were as much a pursuit of emotional and intellectual connection as they were physical. I presume my dearest wife pursued her own alliances outside our marriage, for similar reasons.

While I felt great passion and tender feelings for some of my lovers over the years, sadly, I was never able to find true love as I had when I was much younger. But to my even greater despair, I never had the opportunity to know the love of my own child. Because my wife was unable to conceive, there were no children to dote over or with which to carry on the family name. I did however father an illegitimate child when I was sixteen, but I was never allowed to be part of their life.

My child's mother, who was also the only true love I ever had, was a girl from a nearby village. We met when I was riding through town on my way to meet up with Richard who was on some errand for his brother at the time. We literally came upon each other at a fork in the road.

She was traveling alone on her way to visit a friend who was ailing and bored. I thought her fearless or perhaps daft when she stopped along side of me to say hello and inquire where I might be going. She was a couple of years older than I was, and breathtakingly beautiful. Her long silky dark hair and deep emerald green eyes made it difficult for me not to stare. She also had a smile that made my heart beat so fast, I thought it would burst in my chest.

We just sat in the middle of the road and talked like long lost friends who had suddenly rediscovered one another. I honestly could not say who was chattier, this enchanting girl or myself. To my surprise and sheer joy, she suggested that I rendezvous with her on my way back through town. I knew I should have made some excuse not to, but I was truly smitten and accepted her invitation without hesitation. After we decided upon a day, as well as a time and place, I bid her farewell and continued on my journey.

On my way back from my visit with Richard, who was highly curious and amused by my encounter with the girl, I could not stop thinking about her. When I arrived at our designated meeting spot, I prayed that she did not change her mind. Thankfully, she did not disappoint and arrived only a few minutes after I did.

We could not have picked a more perfect day. The harsh chill of winter was nearly gone. The buds of spring were starting to burst through the ground. Dots of color painted the sparse branches on the trees, offering a welcome end to the gloomy gray vestiges of winter. Warm bright sunshine beamed down from a clear blue sky. The warmth it created on my cheeks felt absolutely wonderful.

We discovered a small relatively soft grassy patch where we could spread out a quilt and sit for a while. It was a lovely spot, close to a creek that bordered a large stretch of farmland and some woods near town. We brought food and drink to share, which we surprisingly seemed to devour like two people who were starving. We ate, talked and laughed for what seemed like hours. As we shared our hopes, dreams and even fears, we held hands and stared deeply into each other's eyes. Before we said goodbye, which I found very difficult, she let me kiss her. It was not my first kiss, but the first kiss that mattered.

I can just picture Richard rolling his eyes at such flowery words and maybe even laughing out loud.

"You are such a romantic," he would often say, almost as if it was an impediment or something I should hide or feel embarrassment about.

But it is who I am. I will never be ashamed of who I am. And let me be frank with you, dear reader. While I may not have had the ideal marriage, my romantic notions and inclinations never left me for want of female companionship or pleasure. I think perhaps, Richard was jealous. And who could blame him?

Returning to my story, it was the most perfect of kisses and I wanted many more of them. To my relief and joy, this delightful girl's desire was in full agreement. I made every possible excuse to rendezvous with her as often as I could. Each time we met, it was harder and harder to say goodbye.

As time went on, we found it difficult to keep our hands off each other and eventually succumbed to our passion for one another. Oddly, she never seemed to worry about her reputation or the consequences of what we did. She simply relished in the pleasure of it all and was hungry for as much as I could give her. And I, being naive, besotted and just as hungry as she was, gave little thought to what might happen if she got with child.

When she realized she was with child, she did not cry, nor did she demand anything from me. She knew I was married to another and that my family's wealth and property were inaccessible to me. She was also keenly aware that my life was not truly my own until I reached my majority. Even then, nothing was truly certain.

Understanding the reality of our times, she recognized how difficult it would be for us to be together even in the best of circumstances. Naturally, I understood that too, but I did not have to like it. I wanted desperately to find a way to be with her, even if it made others around me angry or unhappy.

My first instinct was that I needed to go to my guardian to tell him of my impending fatherhood. I thought that I would plead with him to release me from my absurd marriage contract, which I might add, had yet to be consummated. But this brave and stubborn girl, who held my heart and made me feel truly happy, would not hear of it. She knew that I would be risking a great deal if I angered and disappointed those who were determined to continue benefiting from my sham of a marriage.

"What if I talk to Richard?" I suggested. "Maybe he can reason with his brother the king and get him to make some compromise in our favor."

I practically held my breath as I awaited a response. She hesitated for only a moment and then said "no."

And she was right to do so. It would have only opened the door for disaster and put both her and my child at risk. Their wellbeing was far more important than my own happiness. I listened as she presented her solution, even though my heart ached at the thought of her plan becoming a reality.

Her parents had always wanted her to marry the son of her father's best friend. He was a nice enough lad and had a reasonably handsome face. Though she liked him, she always dismissed the idea of them being together and quickly changed the subject when it arose every so often. But at this critical juncture, she viewed him as the perfect answer to our dilemma. She decided she would marry the boy in haste and let him believe the child she was having was his own.

To protect her secret, I would never be allowed to see my child or have any involvement in his or her life. I was heartbroken at the thought of losing both her and my unborn baby, but she gave me no choice. Her parents, on the other hand, were elated at her sudden change of mind and relieved because she was not getting any younger.

Shortly after she was married, she asked me to meet with her one more time. Unlike our prior rendezvous, this one was brief. A single tear slid down her cheek as she touched her hand to my face.

"I will miss you," she said softly while gazing into my eyes. "Try to be happy" she urged, as if doing so was a simple task one only needed to put a little effort toward.

I was not sure I could ever be happy again, but I told her that I would try and asked that she do the same. Then with a whisper of a kiss on my cheek, she was gone.

One of my greatest regrets is that I never told her that I loved her. I was young, stupid and angry. I think she knew she was important to me. I just hope she knew how much.

Many months after our painful good bye, my sweet, beautiful love gave birth to a baby boy. Having a son who would never know me, and whom I could never claim as my own, left a hole in my heart from that day forward. The only other person who ever knew about this was Richard. We seldom spoke of it, but every now and then it would rear itself like a hot red boil and I would rage about the unfairness of it all. Sometimes, if I were feeling even sorrier for myself than usual, I would cry.

Richard fathered multiple illegitimate children before he married his Anne. But he was not subjected to the same restrictions that I was. He was part of their lives and was able to love and encourage them and ensure their comfort and security. While I was happy for him, I was envious and even angry that I was not permitted the same opportunity.

Thankfully, fate allowed me to catch a glimpse of my son on two occasions. The lad was quite handsome and appeared to be happy and strong. He was the spitting image of his mother, and had a smile that would melt the coldest of hearts. My own heart filled with pride and joy, and immense longing for what I could not have as I watched him and his beautiful mother from a distance.

Tragically, my dear sweet son caught a fever of the lungs and died when he was only eight years old. Not a single day goes by, when I do not think of the precious boy I never had the chance to know. Given the state of things, perhaps it is a good thing that he did not live to see this day.

8

LAW AND RESPONSIBILITY

The chaos of our lives and the world we lived in wore greatly upon us over time. The lack of order was particularly distressing to Richard. Unfortunately, there was little we could do to change things.

While Richard loved and long admired his brother, he became increasingly disgusted with Edward and his unruly reign as the years went by. Debauchery was rampant and on full display for everyone to witness. Edward's gluttony, selfishness, whoring, recklessness and growing disrespect for anyone including himself made Richard sick to his stomach. As such, Richard chose to stay as far away from Edward and the court as possible.

And while he could not control what was happening in London, Richard was determined to do better for the north. And that is exactly what he did.

I suspect the people of the north will always be grateful for his efforts on their behalf.

Richard was unwavering in his intention to bring order wherever he could. Time and again, the only thing that presented itself for this end was the enforcement of the laws of the land. Whether one agreed with them or not, they were the only constant we had.

Laws provided some quantifiable degree of right and wrong. They gave organization or structure to something that operated in absence of these things. More importantly, they gave Richard something to strive for and hold onto.

Some of the more controversial yet nonnegotiable laws we have, grant or deny rights depending on whether or not an individual's mother and father were married before their birth.

Those who are born to legally wedded parents typically receive greater liberty and opportunity than those whose existence is the result of a nonbinding union or illicit affair. The circumstances of one's birth are also among the most important factors in determining who may be in line for the crown.

The law deems that a royal claim requires legitimacy and must also consider gender and birth order. Therefore, if a person is born illegitimate, regardless of whom either or both of their parents may be, they shall have no claim to the throne.

Naturally, many disagree with this rule and others related to legitimacy. However, I do not anticipate any change coming in the foreseeable future. I myself can understand both sides of the argument, but do not feel strongly either way or have any intention of entering into debate on the subject.

Richard, on the other hand, viewed any elimination or bending of these laws to be illogical, and was unwavering in his need to enforce them. The importance of preserving the continuation of dynastic lineage was drummed into him since he was a child. Despite that, Richard never imagined he would have to impose these particular rules of law on his own family.

But when his brother Edward died and the crown was in jeopardy, Richard did what he had to.

Contrary to what others may have thought, Richard never wanted to be king. He never lusted over power as others had. Being keenly aware of the burdens and responsibilities that come with it, Richard also never held any romantic notions about taking on such a role. He simply had a love for this country and its people, and a code that demanded that he fulfill his duty to them.

Until Edward's eldest son reached his majority, Richard would have happily served as Lord Protector[5] as his brother had intended. However, parliament's challenge to his nephew's legitimacy and the volatility of the times left him no choice but to accept the crown.

Parliament issued a document declaring Edward IV's marriage to Elizabeth Woodville to be invalid and any heirs produced from their union to be illegitimate, thereby making their children unworthy to rule. This decision was based on a priest's testimony claiming that Edward had a legal pre-contract of marriage with someone else long before he married Elizabeth.

Even if someone was foolish enough to question the words of a man of God, the woman in question was no longer alive at the time to confirm or dispute the accuracy of this claim. Furthermore, no one could

---

[5] Those who take on the role of Lord Protector, typically do so, during critical times of transition. His primary obligation is to ensure that the business of the kingdom continues without issue and the sovereignty is safe. The Lord Protector also rules or co-rules the kingdom and provides protection and guidance to the underage or ailing monarch he serves. He will perform this duty until his charge is capable of ruling on his own or someone else takes the throne.

produce documentation showing any attempt on Edward's part to dissolve the alleged contract before entering into his marriage with Elizabeth. The fact that he wed in haste and in secret, and without having the banns[6] read, also put his actions under question.

Edward obviously gave little consideration for how any of this may affect his bride and any children they may have. I can only surmise that Edward being king and all, thought it would not matter. I think the only thing he was thinking about at the time was getting Elizabeth into his bed.

You might ask why no one ever questioned Edward's marriage or the right of his heirs before. As I have already indicated, the church communicated their displeasure about not having the banns read. Other than that, I cannot think of any reason for someone to look for damaging information, let alone come forward to challenge the marriage's validity.

I have observed, however, that people tend to scrutinize and question things a great deal more when

---

[6] The reading of banns is an ancient tradition, requiring the parish church of those wishing to marry to announce on three consecutive Sundays their parishioners' intentions to wed. Its primary purpose is to provide an opportunity for others to present objections or legal impediments to the marriage. This custom also allows the community to offer prayers and well wishes to the bride and groom.

there is to be a change in the throne. Individuals who are much further down the royal lineage may choose to discredit those who are ahead of them in hopes of snatching the crown for themselves. While I can only conjecture, I cannot say for sure why this occurred when it did. What I can say is that whether Richard liked it or not, Parliament had spoken and he was our king. As such, he was determined to do everything in his power to warrant the considerable responsibility that was placed upon him.

Once Richard became king, my life became a whirlwind that never seemed to stop. It left me little time to simply contemplate my thoughts and feelings. When I did have one of those rare instances, I found myself almost overwhelmed by the depth of feeling I had. I can recall one such moment that caused me a good deal of uneasiness. It was a time when my political role had greatly expanded and my immediate presence was requested by his royal self.

The carriage ride seemed especially long as I pondered the job that was freshly bestowed upon me. In truth, I had only been a short distance away when Richard summoned me and sent his own carriage to retrieve me. I will have to admit it irked me that he never gave me the option of riding there myself. However, I knew Richard had not meant it to be demonstration of his power or authority, but rather a protective measure and even one of convenience and expediency.

It had only been a few days since my elevation to Lord Chamberlain became official, yet the seriousness and weight of its responsibility lay heavy upon me.

The appointment was not entirely unexpected. After all, Hastings was dead and Richard required someone to take his place. Trust was of the utmost of importance, especially since treachery seemed to be lurking from every corner. Richard had very few people he could depend upon in general, let alone in such an important position. Although I knew Richard trusted and respected me, there was no guarantee that I would be the one he would choose for the job.

I had already been giving council to Richard for quite some time. This new title, however, elevated me to an even more formal and influential role and status that I feared would prove to be more burden than honor. In retrospect, I was right. Although Richard had asked rather than commanded that I take the position, refusing it was not an option for me.

We both shared a vision for this country that we knew could prove difficult to bring into reality. But we were determined to try. As king, Richard would have greater influence and resources available to him than when he was overseeing his beloved north. Despite that, he could not accomplish all that he desired on his own. He needed help.

Richard recognized that I would not be able help him to the level he required unless he placed me high within the ranks. He told me that it was now or never. Hence, dear diary, I jumped in with both feet and eyes wide open. I only wish I would have done so wearing the thickest and sturdiest of boots, and the most solidly constructed armored visor.

I am not usually inclined to brag, but if you will indulge me, I would like to share some of our more noteworthy achievements. In the short time Richard was king, we were able to put in place many new laws and reforms that made things better for the common man.

Richard did not believe a leader of a country should simply collect taxes and live in opulence until the next battle takes place. His perspective of the role of a king was far more expansive.

Unlike others in high authority who valued power and financial gain above all, Richard felt a moral obligation to the people of this land. He believed it was his sacred duty to ensure their peace and add to their comfort and even freedom. While the world was not always inclined to cooperate, Richard was determined to help it along.

The majority of our reforms were made to reduce corruption and promote fairness for our citizens. One of the areas we focused our efforts involved the rights of those individuals who allegedly commit a crime. Allowing for bail, protecting the accused from imprisonment before trial, and preventing forfeiture of goods prior to conviction are examples of some of the improvements we made. We also established minimum property requirements for jurors to lessen the potential for bribery and hopefully allow justice to be better served.

Another one of our more significant accomplishments was the creation of the Court of Requests. Its primary function is to hear the petitions of poor people who cannot afford to seek assistance from the law. Every person who is unlawfully wronged by another, regardless of their financial means, can now have their complaint heard and expect to receive timely resolution according to the laws.

Everyone deserves justice, not just the privileged and powerful. Richard truly believed this. He spoke of this often and was determined to make our legal system accessible to everyone. Therefore, when he had the power to change things, he did just that!

Aside from increasing the potential for justice to be served in our courts, Richard attempted to reduce corruption and unfairness in business and even the government. We enacted laws to protect buyers of land against fraudulent practices, and merchants from unfair foreign competition and trade. We even put in place reforms that would prevent abuse from the monarchy itself by outlawing benevolences, which his brother Edward took advantage of on a regular basis. This ensured that the king could not make demands of the people without them first being sanctioned by Parliament.

Richard's legal actions also took into consideration something that was of personal interest to him. Because he truly loved books, he felt compelled to exempt books and printers from any trade restrictions so that he could promote greater learning in our people.

Also, despite the fact that it had never been done before, Richard was adamant about having the laws published in English. He believed that they should be understood by the people, not just men of the church or nobles who are well versed in Latin or French.

No other king had made the law so accessible to the public. In doing so, it also made it more likely for our citizens to abide by and benefit from them. I ask you, does this sound like the actions of a power hungry, self serving, madman as the Tudors would have you believe? I think not.

Richard's knowledge, interests and even passions were as diverse as his love of people was boundless. He was truly a man ahead of his time. His forward thinking ways and wisdom were evident in the legislation he pursued upon taking the crown. And I suspect as the years go by, his laws will survive and be looked upon quite favorably, even if Richard never gets credit for them.

Sadly, like his hero Arthur, Richard's well meaning and visionary efforts would die with him. But perhaps even more tragically, the world will never know what could have been, had he defeated Henry and lived.

9

A VERY GOOD DAY

Writing about some of the legal successes we had in Richard's brief time as king had me reflecting back to what led to them. Many would consider it rather curious and surprising how much we accomplished in Richard's one and only convening of parliament, let alone how quickly. But what very few people aside from Richard and I knew was that an even greater, yet hidden victory preceded and facilitated our legislative triumph.

This was no small feat, dear reader, but a strategic orchestration of great magnitude. Extensive planning and effort went into making things work in our favor. Every detail was carefully considered and executed, and to our greatest joy, culminated in one of the best days we had ever had. It was truly a glorious day, a day that made us believe that if we were smart enough and worked toward the higher good, anything was possible.

I have tried many a time since Richard's death to think upon and recapture what I felt that wondrous day, so that it could give me the strength and hope to carry on. Sadly, it appears as though my good days are over and all I can do is bask in the glory of the past. Perhaps if I tell you about that shining day, not so long ago, it will turn the tide of luck in my favor once again. I pray that it will be so.

Richard was passionate about many things. But more than anything, he was devoted to upholding the law and bringing order to wherever he could. He also felt a strong need to bring about greater fairness throughout the kingdom, as did I. Assuming one could secure the required consensus, enacting laws could certainly support these objectives. Enforcing them, however, may be another thing entirely.

As I am sure you are aware, human beings are not always honorable. Few can be taken at their word. The fact that inequity is a longstanding aspect of our class oriented society does not help. But even more problematic to higher order causes is that most levels of government are traditionally prone to inefficiency and dishonesty. Therefore, changing our laws would never be enough in such circumstances.

While greed and corruption have always existed, sadly, these things seemed to flourish and grow and become more widespread during Edward's reign. As more and more people abused the power of the offices they held and profited while others suffered, Edward simply turned a blind eye. However, Richard was not his brother. He was determined to put an end to this unacceptable situation or at the very least, lessen its impact and reach. Therefore, when Richard knew he would be made king, our planning began.

Every detail was methodically thought out so we could enact our plan and deliver a decisive blow in total surprise. Even as the targets of our strategic coup gathered, we did not want them to feel even the slightest suspicion or fear a moment too soon.

We asked everyone to gather in London. No one questioned this, because it was where the business of state was generally conducted. Nevertheless, we had an ulterior motive for making them go there. We needed an excuse to get them out of the way in order to collect vital evidence and make changes to fulfill our ultimate objective.

The people we invited were given an important yet ordinary reason for attending. It was widely known that we were already in the process of reforming the court of assesses which involved future property tax obligations. These key individuals knew it was in their best interest to come. They would want to do everything they could to make sure we properly reworked things in their favor. At the very least, they would hope to minimize any negative impact it could have on their current financial situation.

To have sufficient light and time to address issues at hand, we scheduled the meeting to begin first thing in the morning. No one suspected anything out of the ordinary.

Richard and I decided not to use the throne room to address our guests, to reinforce the illusion that nothing was amiss. We chose a large but understated meeting place that seemed better suited to our purposes. The room we selected was long, simply adorned and rectangular in shape. It had a high timbered ceiling and plain wood floors. Dark wood panels covered every wall, except for one side of the room, which was lined with windows.

We even kept Richard's clothing more subdued and business like for the same purpose. No ermine.

No royal robes. Richard wore simple yet elegant dark clothing with jewels of rank as their only adornment. Despite his subtle attire, I told him to wait until everyone was present, so that he could make a royal entrance.

Richard was none too happy. He wanted us to go in together. I knew doing so would diminish the effect we were trying to create. I told him that it would be better if I were already in the room waiting with the others for him to arrive. He knew I was right and begrudgingly accepted my advice.

"It will be alright," I told him as I patted his shoulder to further reassure him. Then just before leaving to join our guests, I cautioned him to refrain from showing any excitement. "Be sure to come in with a sense of power and seriousness," I urged.

He nodded and told me he would do his best.

"I have faith in you," I said, as I headed out the door and made my way to our unsuspecting visitors.

I took my place in the already crowded room to wait for Richard to arrive. I stood with a number of assistants by my side, wearing robes of state as anyone in my position would be expected to wear. My helpers and I situated ourselves just to the left of where Richard would eventually be seated. Behind us, was a long table filled with strategically organized groupings of scrolls and stacks of paper that we would reference during the meeting.

The group of lads who were there to aid me were all rigorously instructed beforehand to conduct themselves in a purely business like manner. They were also cautioned to be silent and attentive and refrain from any smiles or other displays of amusement. These eager young men had to play their roles just as well as Richard and I.

When Richard entered the room, all eyes were upon him. Because I knew him well, I could tell that he was nearly bursting. Inside his head, he was skipping around in circles and shouting "hurrah" or some other celebratory declaration like a child with a favorite new toy. We had already won even before he spoke a single word, but he could not let them know that. Thankfully, he kept his feelings contained and appeared quite kingly and serious. I tried not to make eye contact with him so that neither one of us could be triggered to break out into laughter.

Richard took a seat atop a platform. Even though the chair in which he sat was not a throne, it was still imposing. Green velvet with gold trim was elegantly draped behind him. It not only served to make him stand out in the room, but also gave him a more kingly appearance. The expression he wore on his face was so unreadable, no one expected what was to come.

Once the stage was set, it was finally time to inform those in attendance as to the true nature of why we brought them there. "Gather 'round gentleman," Richard called out to the crowd in the most cheerful of tones. "Come hear your fate."

His smile while speaking appeared genuinely welcoming. No one seemed to suspect that anything truly unpleasant was awaiting them. But all that would change rather quickly. It would not take long before they realized that many of them would lose power. Those who were in charge would no longer be in charge. Moreover, the abuses they so easily made during Edward's time would come to an end.

It would be a day of reckoning for the greedy and corrupt. It would also serve to lay the foundation for having our legislative platform ratified in the upcoming assembly of parliament. By the meeting's end, our captive audience would have every motivation to support our parliamentary agenda despite any prior contrary leanings. Everyone would comply with our wishes if they wanted to avoid suffering any further ugliness.

Many individuals worked tirelessly behind the scenes to make what transpired that day possible. Our loyal and trusted network, most of whom lived and worked in the north, quietly and carefully tracked down the people and information necessary to achieve our success. They also delivered orders to others and carried out orders on our behalf.

Statements were taken. Key individuals were deposed. Vital evidence was uncovered and documented. Properties were reallocated. Everything that could be done to aid our efforts to bring down the people who were in the room with us that fateful day, was done. Had anyone resisted, the details provided in the statements that were collected could have easily been used to influence or coerce them into compliance.

Every alliance and disloyalty was uncovered. We knew who did what and when and where the bodies were buried. And we had every intention to make good use of this knowledge. Every detail was now at our disposal and could be used to our advantage.

With everything out in the open, there was nowhere to hide. While this was a good thing, it also presented us with a challenge. We needed to make sure that the people who were in the room with us that day did not learn of any of this until we wanted them to. Hence, key roads were blocked. Communication channels were restricted. These measures were taken in an effort to ensure that no messages were sent or received by anyone except ourselves and the people who were working on our behalf.

To further secure our position, we cut off support and disassembled the power structures beneath every individual in attendance. Every person who helped them carry out their corruption was replaced. We broke every alliance and cleaned out all the crooked elements we could unearth.

The old structures that fostered unfair practices and abuse were dismantled. Revenue and power would no longer be disproportionate. Anyone who was stupid enough to try to defy us would quickly discover there was no one left to help them.

We had them by their shorthairs. And they had absolutely no idea how we did it.

Everyone in the room stood dumbfounded as each faction was dealt with. Prior to this meeting, we prepared a list of people grouped by their known alliances. We used this as a guideline for sequencing through our agenda. I would announce their names, and then each of them would come forward to hear their fate. My assistants and I provided Richard with copies of land grants, depositions and other supporting documentation, while he informed the relevant parties of changes that had taken place.

Everything was organized beforehand to help us move through every grouping of conspirators quickly and easily. Information was also made readily available to avoid any challenges or questions from going unanswered. Nothing was left to chance. No one suspected that we were going to collect that much documentation against them, let alone in such extreme detail. I imagine they also never expected such an orderly thrashing.

Recognizing how unhappy these men would be with their new circumstances, Richard and I made sure that our people put in place a few key protective measures beforehand. Lands were taken away and redistributed to provide a more trustworthy buffer between those who were loyal and those who were not. Holdings were given to people who could be relied upon to conduct themselves honorably and also be of support to our cause.

We would help those who were loyal by providing them with resources and power to accomplish what they needed and desired. They in turn would help us by guarding strategic roads and informing us of activities in the area. This would allow us to obtain time critical knowledge should something go amiss. We would know rather quickly if corruptive forces were gathering or if there was mustering or escalation or any unusual movements that needed to be counteracted.

All the men who attended that day were blindsided by how quickly and thoroughly we brought them to their knees. They sputtered and squirmed as their worlds came crumbling down before them. No one imagined that we could ever accomplish such a massively complex orchestration, let alone in such a short period of time. They never expected us to be such formidable opponents. All they could do was listen and wait for their very bad day to end.

Our captive audience tried desperately to keep their heads and show a good face in hopes of retaining their land and maybe something more. But it was obvious that their ability to contain their feelings and avoid some outburst would not last much longer.

I am generally a compassionate sort of man and tend to feel sorry for those who are made to suffer by some circumstance. But that day, I had absolutely no guilt or regret for what we put these men through. They were the vilest, most unredeemable of souls who would sacrifice anyone for their own personal gain.

Many of the individuals we brought down that day would go to ground or hide for a while. Some would make every effort to keep out of trouble or at the very least, make it appear that way. Others who were far more evil would get uglier and stoop even lower as time went on.

While the greedy and corrupt lost some footing that day, others were moved toward empowerment and greater personal responsibility. Hope was once again planting its seeds across the land. And while we were cleaning out the undesired elements, we also committed ourselves to righting as many wrongs as we could along the way.

Nobles who were previously pushed to the side by more powerful and crooked individuals were now given their due and allowed to shine and flourish. Many of the loyal hardworking midlevel individuals who helped us were made into new aristocrats and given opportunities they could only dream of. Good people were being elevated and provided with the resources to make a better life for themselves and the people around them.

Our actions destabilized society for the greater good. We made it more equitable and honorable. Now fairness and honesty had a chance to thrive and grow. And we accomplished all of this without any military force, declaration of war or a single drop of blood being spilled.

After the meeting, Richard and I proceeded to pat each other on the back and laugh and shout like children at Christmas who received the best gift ever. With a generous amount of wine and ale, we toasted each other and the good people of England, especially everyone who made that day possible. Then after eating a fine meal, we allowed ourselves to simply relax.

While our efforts delivered a crushing and decisive blow to corruption and evil that day, we knew it was not the end of it. What we had no idea of knowing was that it would unleash a greater and even more cunning evil that would ultimately lead to our downfall. But until then, we allowed ourselves to be happy and grateful for our very good day. Oh how I long once again, for that brief moment in time when light triumphed over darkness, justice and fairness were winning, and the future was ripe with promise. And let me reiterate with pride, there was no war or bloodshed of any manner to make it all possible.

10

FEELING ANGRY TODAY

I realized today that much of my writing seems to emphasize and even glorify Richard's more praiseworthy qualities. I fear, dear reader, that I have given you the impression that I feel nothing but adoration for the man. In truth, there were definitely times I would have enjoyed throttling him until he bled or suffered some crushing pain. I have also thought on more than one occasion of retreating to the Scottish countryside and leaving his royal self to fend for himself.

The man was as stubborn as one could be. He is not the kind of person who gives in to compromise or defers to someone else's perspective too easily. And although his mind perceived things clearly and logically most of the time, he could also be thickheaded on occasion. So much so, it made me wonder if I was dealing with someone with a brain malady. But the thing that bothered me most about Richard was his damn expectations.

Richard had more expectations of others and the world than anyone I know. And God forbid if they were not met, there would be hell to pay. Just like anyone, he liked having his way. He just expected to have it more often than others around him. Having expectations or something to strive for is not bad. But failing to take into consideration others' feelings regarding your expectations is just wrong.

I do not mean to imply that Richard was maniacal or ill intentioned, or that his expectations came out of some sense of royal entitlement. Regardless, it did not make his behavior any less upsetting. I will try as best as I can to explain what I am talking about.

If someone possessed knowledge or skills others deemed valuable or desirable, they were expected to use or demonstrate said abilities on a regular basis, whether they wanted to or not. Richard believed that if you are capable of doing something, you should do it. Just because you can do it, he expected you to do it when he desired it. It became a requirement versus a request or wish.

Richard was polite and never hesitated to express his gratitude when someone did what he wanted. In fact, he was fairly free with his acknowledgment and praise for the good that people would do. People liked being in his favor. It made them feel good and yes valuable. When people are considered valuable, they have less likelihood of being killed or going hungry.

For this reason, people tended to do what Richard asked whenever he asked, and did so without complaint or hesitation. Unsurprisingly, Richard understood this and took full advantage of it. He took it for granted that his expectations and desires would be fulfilled no matter what.

People who desired to stay in his favor would try to anticipate his need and fulfill it without asking. Richard became accustomed to getting what he wanted and assumed his needs would be met without requesting anything of the people in his service.

While he was good at expecting something from others, one could never expect something in return from Richard, unless it suited him. He frequently made excuses, but rarely allowed others to give excuses. Should he actually reciprocate in some way, you counted yourself lucky indeed. That is not to say that Richard was selfish. The man had a truly giving spirit. Unfortunately, he gave a great deal more priority to his own desires and needs than to those who served him.

Because of the circumstances of my childhood, I had to grow up fast and was often on my own. The fact that I was personally motivated, self sufficient, intelligent, logical, capable, honest, good with people and hardworking was very appealing to Richard. Who can blame him? I am rather good if I say so myself. In any event, Richard took advantage of all my vast and favorable qualities. He depended on them. He laid responsibility after responsibility upon me, because I could do it.

Therefore, dearest reader, the more I did, the more he expected me to do. While most of the time I was perfectly happy to do what Richard desired, there were times when I was not. Sometimes I just wanted to be able to say "no Richard," and then without laughter or anger he would tell me "alright Francis."

And even though he bestowed upon me certain honors and material rewards as recognition of my contributions and loyalty, sometimes I felt they were not worth it. Sometimes I felt I would rather be anywhere else than where I was, doing anything else than what I was doing at that moment.

Every now and then, I became weary of it all and just wanted to go home and leave it all behind. I longed to have a normal life and be a normal person whose deeds and words had little bearing on Richard or the state of the kingdom. I yearned to be free of everyone's expectations, especially Richard's.

Richard not only expected me to do whatever he asked, he also expected me to anticipate what he might need or ask in the future and do it without hesitation. While I could take it as a compliment that he trusted my abilities and judgment, sometimes the burden was too much to bear. Sometimes I wanted someone else to be the one who took care of it. I detested having to be responsible and vigilant all the time. There were more times than I care to admit when I would have loved to say, "bugger off Richard and do it yourself."

As good as I was at anticipating and heading off things before they became a problem, I would have appreciated if someone else would have risen to the challenge. I would have also liked to see Richard anticipate some of my feelings and needs and fulfill some of my own expectations once in a while.

Unfortunately, this was not one of Richard's strengths. The truth is, even if I made my feelings known and asked something of Richard rather than hoping for him to guess, it did not mean I would get it. He would frequently claim it was not a good time or that something was of greater urgency or importance that required his attention. More often than not, I would be disappointed and even angry.

Admittedly, there were times when I felt used and so overcome with anger, I would begin to contemplate my escape. But then soon after, I would calm down and remember that despite being in the position of highest authority, Richard was still a flesh and blood human being who was flawed like anyone else. I would reassure myself that Richard cared for me and was the best friend he was capable of being, even if I wanted or deserved better. It is sad to admit, but as disappointing as he was at times, he was by far the lesser of the evils with whom I could choose to be friends.

You may be wondering why I have been dwelling on such unpleasant thoughts today. I have come to the conclusion that I am still quite angry with the man. He left me once again on my own to clean things up and keep fighting as he would expect.

While Richard is relaxing up in heaven, I am stuck here in this chamber. I am alone much of the time and have little with which to entertain myself. I am also feeling painfully uncertain about my future. The current king would love nothing more than to have my head on a stake. And because I do not see anything about my situation changing anytime soon, I am feeling more than a bit angry and despaired.

While the thoughts and feelings of others are important, today I find myself thinking, what about me? I came to the realization that what I want or need has been of little to no concern to anyone else since my father died or maybe never. Even so, after he was gone, it was more than clear that my life became all about how I could benefit everyone else.

I could have easily dwelled on the unfairness, unhappiness and frustration of my circumstances, but I was too busy trying to survive to let myself linger on such things. But it hurt. Even though there were also good times and eventually some benefits thrown my way, it was never enough to take away that hurt. Nevertheless, I do not want to give in to bitterness, but I am allowing myself a single day to just feel sorry for myself. I know doing so will not change a thing, but I do not seem to have much of a choice. So here I sit wallowing in self pity.

Oh poor me, dear diary. Poor Francis.

11

WHAT A NIGHTMARE!

Just like any other child, I would experience the occasional bad dream. While I never liked when that happened, I never really dwelled upon the occurrence or worried about it happening again. But then one day everything changed.

Soon after my father died and I was sent to Middleham, I began to suffer from nightmares with greater frequency. I actually began to dread going to sleep each night. Fortunately, my disturbing nightly intrusions began to lessen over time, and eventually became a rare occurrence, that is until Richard was killed.

Since then, my devoted reader, my already tenuous sleep is intruded upon with greater regularity. I have become so accustomed to these troublesome dreams, I almost welcome them like a visit from an old acquaintance as I drift off to sleep each night.

But I am not feeling quite so hospitable at the present time. Only moments ago, I was ripped out of my sleep after having the most horrific dream I have ever had. My cheeks are still streaked with tears and I cannot stop shaking. Despite my unsteadiness and weakness, I was determined to get myself out of bed. I hobbled over to the table, took a seat and poured myself some wine. Desperate for its calming or numbing effect, I guzzled the liquid down and prayed for some relief. I grasped my quill in my hand and decided to write down what I experienced. My hope in doing so is to never be bothered by such painful thoughts again. However, I fear it will be for naught.

The dream actually began rather pleasantly. I was riding along a country road alone, atop the most magnificent of horses. I was dressed in typical traveling attire and seemed to be in fairly good spirits and health. Just a short distance ahead, I came upon a woman and her child sitting around a fire with their backs towards me.

Suddenly the twosome turned around. To my utter surprise, I realized that the boy and woman were my son and his mother. They smiled and waved, and then asked me to join them. I was so happy to see them. I practically jumped off my horse and rushed to sit beside them near the fire.

I marveled as a gazed upon the girl of my youth, because she was as beautiful as the day we first met. She took my hand and told me how much she missed me. My heart warmed and sped up at her words.

In truth, I never really forgot her. On rare occasions, I even let myself imagine what my life would have been like if we had stayed together. While doing so would give me a temporary feeling of joy, unfortunately, it always ended with a greater sense of pain and loss than if I had not thought of her at all.

As my mind drifted back to happier days, I realized she was saying something important to our son. To my surprise and delight, she told our precious boy that I was his father. At this point, tears of joy were running down my face. My heart was fluttering in anticipation. I was bursting with excitement.

However, my elation was suddenly interrupted as the boy's smile faded and his expression turned angry.

"You are not my father!" he shouted as he glared at me with bitterness in his eyes. "You left me. You did not care about what happened to me. I will never love you. I will never want you in my life. Take your leave now. I can barely look upon you."

His mother tried to calm him down and explain things, but he would not accept anything she said.

She glanced at me with tear filled eyes and whispered that she was sorry as she patted her now weeping son on the back.

I stood up and blinked hard as my body began to shake. Looking back at them one last time, I prayed that everything would be happy and good once again. But it was not to be.

"Go now!" the boy commanded with disgust in his eyes, "Be gone from my sight you pathetic man. You have failed us and you have failed yourself."

His words felt like fire burning through my heart. I fought back the tears as I mounted my horse and rode away. I cried like a tortured animal as I raced along a seemingly endless road to who knows where.

At some point, I came to what looked like an open field. The grass seemed stained and scorched in places and had very little green to it.

As I continued along the road, I began to see piles of arrows, swords, halberds, maces and other weapons strewn about. To my horror, most of these tools of war were splattered in blood and had body parts attached to them. Huge pools of red were also streaked across the road itself in almost a regular pattern.

My eyes began to water and sting from the growing stench of decaying bodies. I started to gag as vomit rose in my throat. Unable to contain my response any longer, I slid off my horse and retched over the blood stained ground.

When there was nothing left to expel, I took a deep unsteady breath and reached inside the bag I had tied to the back of my saddle. I prayed there was something in there to take away the bad taste in my mouth. Before my fingertips were able to latch onto something within the satchel, I was overcome with a piercing pain in my ear. I realized the discomfort I felt corresponded with a sudden, loud noise that seemingly emanated from all around me.

At first, the sound was like thousands of people screaming at the top of their lungs right next to my ear. Then the shrill shouting seemed to stop, but was immediately replaced by a distant chanting. Initially it was so far away, I could not make out what was being said. It was like a soft whisper that drummed on and on. Eventually, the voices appeared to be getting closer, because the words were becoming clearer and louder with each moment that passed. Finally, I recognized that they were saying my name.

"Francis" they said over and over as if searching or pleading. But then the tone turned angry and more desperate, and to be honest, scary. At that point, they expanded their chant to include the word "failure" over and over again along with every variation possible.

"You are a failure. Francis failed us. You failed us. Francis failed me. Francis failed Richard. Francis failed his wife. Francis failed his family. Francis failed his country. Francis failed. We hate you Francis for failing us and failing yourself. You hate yourself Francis for failing."

I covered my ears to try to block the painful words from coming in, but my efforts were for naught. In fact, the more I tried to suppress or ignore the voices, the louder they became. Eventually, the noise became deafening and my ears started to bleed.

Blood oozed down the side of my face and arms and somehow joined with the blood that was already on the ground. The pools of red staining the earth seemed to expand at an alarming rate. As that happened, I heard cheers. Crowds were now celebrating my bloodshed, my anguish. I fell to the ground sobbing, agonizing with pain and despair.

"You are wrong! Your words are not true! It was not my fault," I shouted to the countless nameless voices. "I did not ask for this life, for this burden," I said, and then pleaded with them to stop.

Tears streamed down my face. "Please dear God" I prayed on bended knees, "please help me, help me make it stop."

Suddenly, the tormenting chant became silent, and best of all I felt no pain. I looked around and everything including my horse was gone. No more blood. No weapons. No body parts. No grass. Even the ground was gone. I realized that I was up in the sky standing on a cloud of all things. A huge fluffy white cloud. It felt strangely solid like a stone floor, yet soft to the touch. How funny, I thought.

As I studied my strange new surroundings, I started to wonder if I had died. I felt rather relieved at the thought of being dead. I actually started to laugh about it. It was finally over, I thought. No more pain to endure. No more battles to prepare for, fight or escape from. No more bloodshed. No expectations or pressure. No problems to solve. No more disappointment. Just peace and the ability to just be. I liked the idea. I do not know why I fought so hard to avoid death. It seems quite appealing after all.

Just as I was getting comfortable with my new status, I heard a voice say, "Did you really think it would be that easy? Did you really think you could just put this behind you and be happy and peaceful? No Francis, you are sorely mistaken."

A chill ran up and down my spine. A pain pierced my body where I had been injured at Stoke. The pain intensified and seemed to spread. Then I began to fall. I broke through the cloud rather gently and slowly at first, and then my descent picked up speed. I struggled, screamed, reached and prayed, but I just continued to fall.

Panic and nausea rose inside of me as my body was jostled and spun about in my increasingly rapid descent. I fully expected to hear a large thump and feel my body shatter once it hit the ground. But to my surprise, my fall slowed considerably before the ground was even visible. Then like a feather, I was delicately placed upon the firm earth, standing upright. To say that I was shaken and yet relieved would be an understatement.

As I tried to slow my breathing and calm myself, I realized I was not alone. Crowds of people were lining a village street on which I suddenly found myself standing. Some were shouting, while others chose to whisper among themselves. More than a few were laughing, as an even greater number wept with such despair, I felt quite sorry for them. Most however, simply looked on, waiting silently for something or someone to appear.

I stood there searching the countless faces that surrounded me, as well as the dust filled road they gathered along for some explanation. Then to my horror, I finally saw what they were all waiting for. A man's naked, war torn body was draped over a horse with a sword shoved into his backside and on display for everyone to see.

Oh God, Oh God, I thought, as it became obvious to me that the ill-treated corpse was what was left of Richard. I heard that they paraded him around to show he was defeated, and to prove he was dead and that Henry was their king. They defiled his body. They wanted to humiliate him even in death. I could not bear to look further.

"Why are you making me see this?" I asked, gazing up at the sky with tears streaming down my face.

After a long silent pause, I heard the words, "because you failed Francis!" Then I woke up.

12

DEFINING MOMENTS AND PAIN

Thanks be to God, dear diary, I was able to sleep through an entire night without a single bad dream. In fact, I had no dreams at all and had the best sleep I have had in years. To say that I am relieved after having such a horrible dream the night before, and very little rest for such a long time, would be a supreme understatement. That is not to say that the effects of said nightmare have left me completely. In fact, I find myself pondering every detail of my dream over and over in an attempt to put it behind me once and for all.

The theme of yesterday's dream was undoubtedly disturbing and even surprising on many levels. Most notably, it has not escaped me how much responsibility I have allowed myself to take on regarding my departed friend and king. Despite knowing that Richard's death is not my fault, it is clear that I carry some burden and even guilt for it.

Perhaps it is the pain of losing someone important to me and the powerlessness in not being able to prevent it from happening that bothers me the most. On the other hand, maybe failing to obtain retribution somehow makes me responsible, and thus destined to be without peace until I can achieve it. I can only venture to guess.

Obviously, I cannot change the past. Regrettably, after our recent failed attempt, any potential to defeat Henry and bring him to justice has diminished so significantly, there appears to be little reason to try.

Even if there are others like myself who want things to be different, very few are still alive and willing to risk anything more to help in this effort. And lest we forget, my own body is not exactly eager to submit itself to additional punishment regardless of how noble the cause may be. Therefore, challenging Henry at this point or anytime in the near future would be highly problematic, if not impossible.

Without any chance or means to take away the crown from our current and undesirable king, I am truly at a loss as to how to remedy my predicament. I do wish dear diary you could respond to what I am writing and advise me on such a matter. But alas, you are simply paper and ink, and I am on my own.

In pondering my current circumstances, I realize that so much of my past has brought me to where I am today. It also unfortunately makes going forward even more difficult.

I do not know anyone who has not been changed or haunted by some defining moment in their life. A sudden death, illness, loss of livelihood or a dream that can no longer come true can make anyone uncertain and less hopeful about the future. These experiences could also forever alter the course of a person's life and become their greatest detriment to happiness.

For many, the most painful times involve loss or separation from someone with whom they were close or something that gave them comfort. I have seen time and again that even the strongest of souls can be tested in times of loss, no matter what they do.

When Richard's son and only legitimate heir died, it shook him to his core and he could barely speak. He seemed so fragile and defeated. I did not know if Richard's heart would ever recover. I did not know if I would ever see him smile again. Then when his wife

Anne became ill and eventually died, Richard became totally inconsolable. His grief was more than he could bear. I truly think part of him died when they did. It was so difficult to see him like that and not be able to do anything to make it better. Despite his pain, he eventually surprised me with his ability to garner the strength to go on.

I believe it was a combination of faith and Richard's personal sense of honor and duty to something greater than himself that allowed him to continue and look towards the future. However, dearest reader, the man I knew was never truly the same. The light in my dear friend and king was ever dimmer.

I often wonder what Richard was thinking that fateful day, as he faced tremendous betrayal and then impulsively charged his horse toward Henry and ultimately met his demise. I suspect he was quite angry, and justifiably so. But I truly think he was wrestling with something more. Something that challenged his very core.

When one cannot count on the people around them, and the people they care about keep dying, it is easy to lose hope and any reason to keep trying.

Confronted with such a painful reality, it is not hard to see why someone would give up.

While I will never know what he was thinking or feeling that day, I do hope Richard has finally found some peace. I know that I would be extremely grateful if I could find some peace, preferably sooner than later, and before I have to leave this world. I pray that the pain and disappointment of the past will not be in the forefront of my mind in my final moments. At the very least, I would like to have a few more restful nights of sleep similar to the one I just had.

13

TRUTHS AND OTHER REVELATIONS

I think it is more than clear, dear reader, that the man who was both my friend and king was not perfect by any means. Despite that, he always tried to be the best he could.

Richard held a unique and idealistic view of the world and strived to use any power he had to make it a better place. As I have alluded to in my earlier entries, unlike most of the people around him, he lived by a code and valued honor, loyalty, family and God above all things.

Richard never made his views and priorities a secret. Yet surprisingly, their significance was often minimized. Moreover, people frequently spouted generalizations and lies that showed that they did not really know him at all. Even people who knew him well had not understood the degree in which his code ruled the decisions he made.

What people did not know was that he was also influenced by something outside of his beloved code that would probably shock you. He called them "knowings" and described them as sporadic glimpses into certain truths and future potentials.

While I do not think anyone could confuse Richard with a prophet or wizened seer from the bible, surprisingly, these glimpses generally proved to be accurate. As such, Richard learned early on not to dismiss them. Given the delicate nature of this unusual ability, only Richard's wife, his childhood nanny and I knew about it.

I know what you are thinking. If he knew things before they occurred, did he know he was going to die? And if so, why did he go there to fight Henry if he was destined to lose? The answer is no.

Richard had no idea what was to happen to him. Unfortunately, his "knowings" were rarely if ever about himself. They were also frustratingly infrequent or poorly timed, and never appeared upon request. They would come on suddenly and strongly like a rock that breaks loose from a hillside and unexpectedly makes contact with someone's head. Much like a rock, he could not ignore them. They would plague him until he acknowledged them and acted upon their urgings in some way.

I cannot tell you how many times Richard looked into my eyes and said in the most solemn of tones, "Because I know Francis. I just know."

And because I knew Richard, I believed him. I only wish that Richard's "knowings" would have made an exception that fateful day and spared him his life.

Richard's "knowings" along with information gathered from carefully placed spies played a significant role in his leadership in an attempt to prevent as much disaster as possible. It also aided us in making our "Very Good Day" a reality. The times we lived in were challenging at best. Given that adversity and chaos seemed to sprout from every corner on a daily basis, we needed any help we could get.

This brings me to the topic of his nephews. As you know, Edward's eldest son, also named Edward was expected to take the crown after his father's death. Richard was assigned by his dying brother the role of Lord Protector to help the young king until he reached his majority.

Even before preparations began for the coronation, Richard became aware of numerous plots against the boy who would be king. The prince's deliverance to London was hastened so that he could be better protected. Guards were assigned to watch over the lad day and night while he stayed in the tower.

Not too long after, Richard heard rumors that his other nephew, Edward's younger brother Richard, was also in danger, even though he was not first in line for the throne. Someone was quickly dispatched to bring him to London to join his brother, so both of the boys could be closely watched.

As you also know, after the parliament declared Edward IV's marriage invalid and his heirs illegitimate, Richard became king instead of his brother's son. Surprisingly, the rumblings of plots against his nephews did not cease. In fact, the threat to these children appeared to be getting bigger, almost as if Richard was irrelevant.

Intriguingly, Richard's "knowings" also occurred with greater frequency at that same time. Because every piece of information he was getting from his spies coincided perfectly with what he was already feeling, he believed danger was truly imminent. Determined to keep his brother's children safe, he decided to have his nephews moved.

Because there were so few people he could trust, Richard delegated the task of finding a new and safe location for his brother's sons to me. Because allegiances changed by the day and new threats developed over time, we actually moved the boys on several occasions as a precautionary measure.

Only Richard and I knew where his nephews were at any given time. Only a handful of people knew they were in hiding and being moved for their safety. Elizabeth Woodville was one of the few who were aware of Richard's efforts on behalf of her sons. Because she was their mother and a woman who understood the reality of our times, she kept the knowledge to herself.

Then when rumors and allegations surfaced suggesting that the princes had met some sinister end, Richard was forced to choose between public opinion and his nephews' safety. Having already lost so much by this point, he could not allow any further losses to occur especially on his watch. He was determined to protect those boys, even if it cost him.

Despite the growing pressure to produce some evidence that the princes were still alive, Richard stood firm. He would never bring the boys out into the open if there were even the slightest chance that they could be killed.

His loyalty to his family and his oath to protect them was far more important than his own reputation. As the dynastic head of the family, Richard also felt obligated to ensure the continuation of the line and the safety of everyone who may be part of it. This even included Elizabeth Woodville.

Prior to confronting him on the battlefield, Richard had a "knowing" that Henry was planning to have his nephews killed and already dispatched men to find them. He also knew that Henry planned to marry Richard's niece Elizabeth if he was successful at killing Richard and taking the crown. Then to make his union more valid and powerful, he knew Henry would issue a royal decree shortly after taking the crown, to legitimize Edward's marriage to Woodville. Doing so would make their daughter, his bride, legitimate as well.

The only problem with this scenario was that it would make Edward's son once again first in line for the throne. It would also make Henry's reign invalid. Logically, for Henry's plan to work out the way he intended, he would have to eliminate the princes. Richard knew Henry would not wait until he had the crown to do it. Although Henry would have sent his men to kill two boys, there was actually only one prince alive at that time. Sadly, the youngest of Edward's sons perished from some affliction of the lungs some time ago.

Richard was desperately afraid about someone discovering his remaining nephew's location. He actually instructed me to move the boy one more time before he left to face Henry and unfortunately met his death. I have actually moved the lad several more times since my friend was killed.

Had Henry been defeated instead of Richard, the boy would have eventually been able to come out into the open. Unfortunately, that never happened. Therefore, young Edward will have to stay where he is. The person with whom the prince was left in their care pledged to keep the boy safe and ensure that he never tells anyone his true identity. While I have revealed that the boy still lives, nothing short of Henry's death will cause me to divulge his whereabouts.

As I write about all of this, I find myself once again reflecting back to how Richard dealt with Hastings. Although Richard never said this to me, aside from the obvious betrayal, I think perhaps the real reason he was executed so quickly was that Hastings knew too much. His disloyalty, combined with the secrets he was privy to, put everyone and everything Richard cared about at risk. Richard did not kill the man out of hatred, spite or hurt. He killed him to protect his own.

I have yet one more secret to reveal. Everyone thought that I fought in the battle that claimed Richard's life. Despite that, no one remembers seeing me there or has any inkling as to what happened to me. They just assumed I had been there and got away. Admittedly, I fed this belief by never denying it. I also added to its acceptance by doing something that convinced my own wife to think that I was there.

Soon after learning of Richard's death, I made a will of sorts, using a date that preceded the battle even though it was written afterward. I asked a trustworthy contact to deliver this document to Anne in haste. I hoped to ensure that she would be taken care of in the event of my death.

Although I was perfectly happy to have people believe that I fought against Henry that day, I never went there in the first place. The truth is Richard did not want me there. Being one of his closest friends and advisors, Richard thought that I was far too important to be put in harm's way. Regardless, he honestly did not think he would need my help. He much preferred that I attend to other matters while he put an end to Henry once and for all.

Having me elsewhere was a common theme with Richard. Case in point, Richard asked me to coordinate sending men to the southern coast of England near South Hampton in hopes of preventing Henry from landing there. He did not wish me to go there personally. Richard just wanted me to make it happen and keep apprised of any developments.

Unfortunately, Henry entered the country through Wales, so this effort was for naught. This is another one of those moments that I find myself thinking much too frequently about. Had Henry actually showed up in the waters near Hampton as the rumors suggested, we could have dispensed with him before he even made land. Then Richard would be alive today and I would not be writing you this long and depressing tale.

I can remember the last time that I saw him as if it were yesterday. He seemed calm and acted like it was just an ordinary day. Richard assured me that he was feeling completely confident about his upcoming battle and patted my shoulder and smiled as if to emphasize the point. He then hesitantly admitted that I was left out of it as a precaution. He wanted to ensure that I lived and could not be tortured for what I knew, should the unimaginable occur.

I have often questioned in my head Richard's true motivation in his decision to go without me. His choice could have been as he said, he was merely being cautious. On the other hand, perhaps he had a "knowing" that something bad was going to happen and just refused to acknowledge it. I wish I knew. Even more so, I wonder if the outcome would have been different, had I been there. Maybe my presence would have prevented him from impetuously charging headlong into danger. I guess dear reader we will never know.

14

FIGHTING ON

You have probably asked yourself, dearest reader, why in heaven's name would anyone who has lost almost everything continue to fight on? I have asked myself the same question multiple times. The answer is always the same and simpler than one would imagine. Because I could.

I suspect you believe me to be daft or someone with a strong death wish or a lust for blood maybe. Although there have been times when I wondered if I might be crazy, I am fairly certain I am of sound mind on most days. Moreover, I have never found joy in the killing of another, even if they deserved it. And despite not having much to live for, I have always regarded life as a precious gift from God. As such, I am resolved to go on living until the good Lord sees otherwise.

You may be wondering, what about revenge? I am not going to lie to you. I was very angry. I still am. Going after Henry for the simple pleasure of enacting revenge certainly had its appeal. It still has. God knows the slimy arse deserves it.

I know you may find what I am about to say hard to believe. But despite the immense satisfaction I would get from killing the odious swine for what he did to Richard, my motivations for challenging him were more altruistic. I wanted to make sure that Henry never had the opportunity to destroy all that Richard and I worked hard to put in place. I also wished to preserve some semblance of honor and sanity in the world in which I lived, and provide a better future for England and its people.

While there were times when I could have easily given up and run away to some distant land and begun anew, something deep inside of me would urge me to stay and fight. That something was hope.

Even though some thought it to be a lost cause, I and others like myself still saw a potential for Henry to be defeated. Whatever the risk or likelihood of success, we were determined to try. Unfortunately, we lacked agreement as to what we would do if we were lucky enough to remove Henry from the throne and kill the usurper once and for all. We were however, united in our determination to prevent him from further enjoying the spoils of his newly acquired and undeserved position.

Within the two year period following Richard's death, I spent much of that time in hiding, seeking out information and planning for my next step. More recently, as you know, there was the added challenge of having to heal my body after battle.

The most frustrating and overwhelming part of my situation was enduring constant uncertainty and having to wait long periods of time to learn or act upon something. Such circumstances made it quite easy to dwell on negative thoughts and give in to doubt and fear. It was also bloody hard to muster up the enthusiasm to fight as others who tried to overthrow Henry failed in their attempt. The fact that it became more difficult to reach Henry as he consolidated power did not help. But no matter how bleak things appeared, I was determined to keep trying. I just hoped my efforts would have proven more fruitful.

15

BAD NEWS AND HARD CHOICES

I tried to keep my mind busy, while I awaited news of what I hoped would be Richard's defeat of Henry. Thankfully, I had a large stack of papers to read through to help pass the time. Richard requested that I review them so we could discuss them when he returned.

Unfortunately, I felt my focus waning as the day stretched longer without any word. My fingers started to drum nervously against the top of my desk as my mind began to wander. Most of my thoughts were trivial and fairly positive at first, but grew darker as the minutes went by. I shook my head, as if the act would create a more hopeful shift in my thought processes.

My attention was suddenly distracted by a young monk bursting into my chamber. The boy man that stood in the doorway was covered in dust, splattered in blood, and looked weary and unsteady on his feet.

I rushed to his side to give him some support and lead him to a chair before he could fall. Pressing a cup into his trembling hand, I then urged him to drink up before trying to speak. He guzzled the liquid down like someone who had thirsted for days.

It was clear that he was here to report of the battle. Monks oftentimes provide one of the few surviving witness accounts to war. They are frequently seen administering to the wounded and providing water to those who have fought. While these men may have loyalty to a particular side in a conflict, their first loyalty is to God and the injured. No one will typically attempt to harm these men because of this reason. Although they may walk away with their bodies intact, I wonder how the horrors they have witnessed have affected their minds and spirits.

The young man who sat before me looked so fragile. I nervously searched his face for a clue. The pit of my stomach tightened as I recognized both sadness and fear in his eyes. I silently reassured myself in my head that it meant nothing and that everything was okay. The lad nodded and thanked me, and then proceeded to tell me what he was tasked to travel a full day on foot to tell.

"All is lost," he said, almost in a whisper, as his voice cracked and his eyes began to water. "The king is dead. You must make haste and flee. You are not safe here."

When I heard the news of Richard's defeat and death, my initial response was to relegate it to nothing more than a cruel fabrication. I could not comprehend how it could possibly be true. But dear reader, this was no taunting falsehood created to fulfill someone's twisted amusement, revenge or political aspirations. The monk who brought me the troubling report did not share hearsay, but rather what he had personally witnessed. Despite his reluctance to speak of it, the truth however terrible had to be told.

My dear friend and king was gone, along with his hopes and dreams for the future. No matter how much I wanted it to be otherwise, I had to accept the fact and move forward as best as I could.

The young monk was right. I needed to go where I would be safe. I also needed to have some time to clear my head and decide what to do. However, the initial shock, pain and anger I felt was so overwhelming, it made it difficult for me do anything in that moment. I was totally incapable of forming any logical thought in my mind, or moving or acting with any degree of stability, reason or speed. My insides twisted turned and ached, and my body trembled as I stood in silence trying to come to some understanding of what had happened.

As the lad continued to provide bits and pieces of what occurred, I felt as if a thick fog had enveloped my mind and made everything around me, and everything I thought I understood, distant and obscured. It was becoming increasingly difficult to focus on what the monk was saying, let alone contemplate the implications of what he told me. But then suddenly, my mind snapped back into clarity. I was once again connected to the reality of that moment. As that happened, I realized it was not just my safety that was of urgency but that of Richard's nephew.

Young Edward was in the other room and under my protection and charge. No matter how upset I was, I had to garner the strength to do what was necessary for the sake of the boy. It was what Richard expected and wanted, and what I pledged to do. And grief be damned, praying that the Almighty give me the strength and guidance I needed, I set out to do just that.

I know this may be hard to understand, but despite being a fugitive on the run, in some ways I was still in power. Although someone else had declared himself king, the government and all that we established before them was essentially still in place. The fact that Henry's victory was fresh, and that he had neither the time nor resources to put his own people into place yet, provided a brief advantage. Even more importantly, a whole network of loyal supporters who did not fight or perish with Richard still existed, and thus could be called upon for assistance.

While a gaping and painful hole had been created with the death of my friend and king, all was not truly lost. What we created and what was at risk was much bigger than Richard. The work we started needed to continue without him. How, I was not sure. But as long as I had a heartbeat, I was determined to pursue every option until we have won or I was dead.

Despite the fact that it would take longer, just like the monk who gave me the terrible news, young Edward and I would initially travel by foot. Doing so would make it less likely for us to attract attention, and would also give us greater ability to hide should the need arise.

After temporarily securing the boy in a safe place, I set out to do two things. Staying alive and avoiding capture was obviously my highest priority.

I did everything I could to keep Henry and his men chasing their tails, not knowing if I were among the living or dead. I also kept them guessing where I might turn up and what I might do next. To facilitate this purpose, I never stayed in one place too long. I traveled in a variety of directions with no consistent or recognizable pattern. More importantly, I fueled rumors by leaving a trail of false information at strategic locations to make Henry think what I wanted him to think.

One of my more elaborate and effective deceptions involved Colchester. Because it was what I wanted them to believe, many assumed that I took sanctuary there at St. John's Abbey. While most churches offered a maximum of forty days of safe haven and protection for political, as well as criminal fugitives, St. John's policy was far more generous. It would afford someone like me as much time as they wanted to come to a decision and put into place some plan of action. Also, given that they have long been supporters of the Yorkists, it would be considered a logical place for me to bide my time.

While I did actually go to St. John's, my time there was extremely brief. I only stayed long enough to secure the illusion that I wanted to achieve.

My plan had many facets to it. The most critical part involved letters that were written and signed in my own hand prior to my even arriving there. I handed a stack of them to the Abbot and instructed him to send them out at specific intervals. The idea was to make it seem as if I was still residing there. As I was presumably pondering potential options for my future, it would be logical for me to conduct inquiries and correspond with others to determine my next step. To add to the effect, I also had some of my local contacts feed rumors to support the perception of my being there for a lengthy sanctuary stay.

Thankfully, the Colchester ruse provided the perfect distraction so that I could move about more freely and attend to my second objective. While I was doing all that I could to subvert the attention and efforts of my enemy, I was also making inquiries to assess current attitudes and support to determine my next course of action.

Laughably, Henry and others thought I was actually considering taking a pardon and helping him transition the kingdom to his favor, while I allegedly took refuge in Colchester.

Such a ridiculous notion for Henry to think I could forget everything that has happened and sacrifice everything I believe in to aid him after he killed my friend. He would be crazy to believe I could do such a thing, just to save my head and keep a portion of my vast properties and financial resources. That, my dearest reader, is not who I am.

Even if I was stupid, scared and maybe greedy enough to agree to loathsome Henry's terms, I know things would not have worked in my favor. I have no doubt that once he gleaned all that he could from me, he would not hesitate to take my head and all my worldly possessions. I cannot blame the man for trying. Desperate times call for desperate measures. Sorry Henry, but I cannot be bought.

While donning a variety of disguises, I zigzagged and went every which way across England to keep Henry's men at bay and gather information. During my travels, I circled back to pick up Richard's nephew and deposit him in another presumably safe location. I moved him a few more times until I felt he was truly secure. After that, I could finally focus my attention on what to do about Henry.

As I discussed before, much of what Richard and I put in place was still in place. Unsurprisingly, many who were loyal to Richard and perhaps fought alongside of him were dead or in less than desired circumstances. However, there were still a considerable number of men alive and well, and highly motivated to remove the Tudor usurper from the throne. Unfortunately, everyone was scattered about and justifiably scared.

Coordinating efforts and constructing and implementing a plan under Henry's nose without him finding out was difficult to say the least. But even more challenging was the broad lack of agreement as to how, when and where, along with what to do if we were successful in overthrowing Henry.

Our greatest dilemma was the lack of a clear figurehead to inspire people to rally around and fight for. As I have indicated before, Richard had no living legitimate heir and the illegitimacy of Edward's heirs was still a problem. George's heir was legitimate, but many excluded him from consideration for the throne because his father was found guilty of treason and executed. People also dismissed the boy as a viable option because of some concerns regarding his mental and emotional state and ability to serve.

Richard's sisters, on the other hand, had children that could potentially fulfill our purpose. However, aside from the fact that people tended to frown upon heirs from a maternal line ruling, we could not be sure if any of them would want to. Even though we did not have all the answers, many of us were still willing to lay down our lives because the alternative was too horrible to accept.

There were actually multiple rebellions or planned attacks on Henry in the works. Most were being organized in the north, where Richard was so beloved, and where many of the people who lived and worked there hated Henry. I met with many individuals in secret to discuss strategies and garner support.

In an attempt to win the favor of the people or if unsuccessful, scare them into compliance, Henry was rumored to be heading north. When word reached us about his plans, my fellow Yorkists saw this as an opportunity.

"Tis a sign, my brothers! God is bringing him to us," one of my associates declared with the biggest of grins. "We shall answer to Lord and smite Henry, and the Lord and the people of the north shall rejoice!"

"Let it be so!" others in the room shouted as they lifted their eyes toward the sky.

Part of me wanted to tell these men they were being foolish, but I chose to stay silent to avoid risking offending someone or even worse snuffing out hope. While I prayed that we had the Lord's favor, I doubted it would make a difference. I could not help but think that if God was truly on our side and against Henry, Richard would still be king and Henry would be dead. Obviously, thinking and saying such things would not be beneficial to achieving our goal.

I decided to imagine that God had either changed his mind or was distracted by another important matter when Richard was defeated and killed. I chose to believe that he was now totally focused and firmly on our side and available to help in any way he could.

Deluding one's self is not the best thing to do. But sometimes, it may be the only thing one can do to avoid giving up or running away. I was not ready to abandon hope so easily. As such, I plodded forward with my faith in an illusion and hoped that the Lord Almighty was willing to comply and make it a reality.

As I mentioned before, there were a number of groups and strategies in play. No one was willing to change their plan and consolidate efforts into one strategic attack. The thought was that multiple actions would allow a chance for at least one to succeed should any of the other plans fail. I was not quite sure if I agreed with this perspective, but had little chance of changing people's minds about this. Given how things turned out, I often wonder what would have happened if we had combined our efforts.

I must point out, however, Henry did not suffer from a lack of resources or support despite his tenuous and stolen rise to power. He had a loyal group of followers and even more significantly a network of spies at his disposal who were ruthless and seemingly willing to do anything for their liege.

Truth be told, no one could be truly certain as to whom they should trust, regardless of which side they were on. With such precarious circumstances, there would be no telling how successful we would have been even with a larger and more consolidated plan. Just as Richard was betrayed, there was no guarantee that any of us who were trying to take the crown from Henry would not suffer the same fate.

One group of men came the closest to killing Henry. Their actions were haphazard at best. Their lack of planning and poor timing made their efforts doomed from the start. If only luck would have been on their side. But it would seem luck was elsewhere at the time. As disappointing as their result was, other attempts to overthrow Henry were also unsuccessful.

Unfortunately, as expected, this one group's near miss led to increases in Henry's security detail, making it even more difficult for anyone to get close to him. This also served to fuel Henry's anger and strengthen his desire for immediate revenge.

Regardless of someone's participation or lack of involvement in the attempt on his life, if they were perceived to be a danger to Henry's future, they were taken out. While I was able to escape discovery and retribution, others were not so lucky.

Sadly and unsurprisingly, Henry took out his rage on anyone he could get his hands on. Many a good man died because of it. Most were killed quickly and somewhat honorably. However, he decided to make a special example of one of the leaders of a group, which focused their efforts further southwest.

Henry's message was clear. Anyone who might be inclined to challenge him in the future should think twice about it if they did not want to end up like Humphrey Stafford.

Humphrey took a much bolder approach to dealing with Henry than the rest of us. He did not work toward his goals in the shadows, but rather walked the streets like a free man without a care in the world. When he encountered someone who knew of his prior loyalties and questioned his current allegiance, Humphrey simply declared that Henry had already given him a pardon. Unsurprisingly, not everyone believed his lie even though he behaved as though he had nothing to fear.

In the public view he lived a facade, but behind the scenes, he schemed with his brother and others to kill the same man he pretended to support. Tragically, Humphrey's gamble went dreadfully wrong. Despite what many judged to be recklessness on his part, none of them believed it warranted such an extreme response. He simply did not deserve what Henry did to him.

The poor man was forcibly taken out of sanctuary and condemned to a barbaric traitor's death. They hung him, but cut him down before he was dead. Then while Humphrey was still alive, they castrated and disemboweled him, all the while burning his insides in front of him. As if that was not bad enough, they beheaded and quartered his body. His head was tarred and set atop a spike over London Bridge for all to see. The other bits of him were also tarred and then displayed in a variety of towns where he was well known. God rest his poor soul.

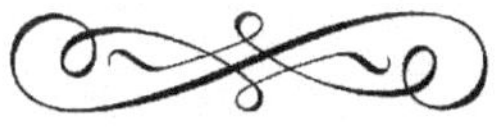

16

ONE LAST CHANCE

My one and only true attempt to put an end to Henry began as a conversation between a boy, his teacher, Richard's nephew John de la Pole, Earl of Lincoln, and myself. The meeting occurred upon the request of Richard's sister Margaret, Duchess of Burgundy. One of her trusted contacts suggested a few months earlier that the boy and his teacher might be beneficial to our cause.

After conducting further inquiries, Margaret decided that an alliance may indeed prove to be advantageous. But she wanted to be sure. She asked her nephew John and myself to meet with them in person to determine if our shared interests could actually lead to a solid plan for overthrowing Henry.

Margaret knew I would never say no to her, especially if there was any chance of taking back our kingdom. John on the other hand was more of an uncertainty. Because he already pledged his loyalty to Henry and was not typically receptive to causing any trouble, no one could be sure what he would do.

To be clear, his allegiance was out of fear rather than admiration or loyalty. John never forgot that this man killed his uncle and other family members and friends. However, he was not eager to take the man on. He was committed to playing the game in order to keep himself and the people he cared about out of harm's way.

John had little patience and fondness for Henry's handling of things since taking the crown. Despite that, it would take a lot for him to sacrifice his life to do anything about it. But because he also respected his aunt and did not want to disappoint her, he agreed to the meeting.

My curiosity was certainly piqued at the time, but I had no expectation regarding the outcome. John, on the other hand, had little confidence that anything would come of our discussions with the boy and his teacher. Both of us were truly surprised by what awaited us.

My first impression when arriving at our secret meeting place was that this boy, who called himself

Lambert Simnel, looked amazingly like Edward's eldest son. They were nearly identical in appearance. Had I not known that Richard's nephew was safely hidden and far away, I would have thought that he was standing before me. But it was obvious with a second look that this boy was clearly younger than the prince I know. Even so, I was quite startled in those first few moments.

I was also impressed by the boy himself. He exuded confidence and was extremely intelligent, well spoken and wonderfully calm and cheerful in his demeanor. I cannot imagine anyone not liking the boy straight away.

During the course of our discussion, the Simnel lad offered up a proposal that he and his teacher conceived in the months prior to our meeting. This plan would eventually become the foundation for a complicated and dangerous undertaking. Most notably, it was an endeavor that would put the boy himself squarely in the line of fire.

The scheme required that Lambert would pose as the son of Richard's late brother George. The original thinking was for him to pretend to be Edward's eldest son, because they looked so much alike. However, it was later decided that George's son would be received with greater credibility given that there was more recent talk about him than any of Edward's sons.

Stories of George's son being imprisoned in the tower were rampant as were tales of his secret execution. Our young pretender would serve to prove the rumors to be false and put Henry on the defense. It would also be viewed as a hopeful sign by the Yorkist's cause. Because most of the participants in our ultimately failing venture were unaware of the deception, the lad would become the most important motivating force in our effort.

People are not generally inclined to fight if they have no one to fight for. Lambert gave our cause what it needed, a person troops could rally around. His presence provided the final and most essential piece for any potential plan for defeating Henry to succeed.

I will admit our strategy to confront Henry at Stoke and more specifically, the use of Lambert, was ill conceived. But the boy was critical of Henry and found the idea of tricking and scaring him and ultimately leading to his demise to be utterly amusing, as did his teacher.

I would be lying if I said that I was unreceptive to another chance at ending the foul usurper once and for all. However, I did not like the idea of a mere boy being made the sacrificial lamb to do so. But this boy believed strongly in our cause and was determined to help.

I asked him plainly, "are you sure you want to go through with this?"

I was determined to put an end to this perilous plot if I witnessed even the slightest bit of hesitancy from the boy. To my surprise, he looked into my eyes with an unmistakable resolve that he knew what he was doing and responded instantly with a simple "yes."

Many would consider Lambert's conviction to be a sign of immense bravery. Others would call it stubbornness or perhaps foolishness. As for myself, I viewed this boy's actions to be a clear indication of his commitment to something higher than himself. I recognized within him a deep sense of loyalty and a damn code that he needs to uphold even if he has to die for it. Sound familiar?

Thankfully, despite being a total imposter with no royal claim, the lad was truly talented in making people believe otherwise. Of course, it also helped that the boy's teacher devoted many months before our meeting tutoring him in courtly manners and ways.

Understandably, there were some doubts as to whether Lambert could truly pull off the deception. We comforted ourselves in the knowledge that people always believe what they want to believe. Therefore, despite the risk and the sick feeling and pain I had in my stomach, we agreed to go forward with the plan.

Once an agreement was reached, John and I contacted our most trusted associates. We instructed them to gather as many people as they could find who were still loyal to the Yorkist cause and encourage them to fight. Margaret helped in spreading the word and also provided resources that were critical for us to succeed. Most significantly, she gave us much needed financial support and even hired almost two thousand German mercenaries and their captain to fight with us.

Support for our attempt to overthrow Henry grew rapidly. It was however unclear as to how many of those who encouraged our efforts would actually show up to fight. We hoped we would have enough men along with the right strategies to succeed, and prayed that weather and God's mercy and protection would be on our side.

To invigorate our supporters and bring strength to the illusion we were trying to create, the Simnel boy was crowned before we engaged Henry in battle. The ceremony took place in Ireland. The location was chosen for its safe distance from Henry, but more importantly because of the Irish's opposition to Henry and strong support for the Yorkists.

It was truly a boon for our cause that Irishmen and Germans were choosing to fight with us. Many regarded their support as a sign from God that he wanted us to dispense of Henry. Given that Henry prevailed and many who fought against him have died, it makes me think otherwise.

In any case, once Lambert was crowned king and strategies were agreed upon and finalized, it was time to put the plan into action. Back to England we went, resolute to face our enemy head on and defeat him once and for all. Confidence and hopes were high. Unfortunately, as you know, things did not work out in our favor.

We did have some victories early on that made us think that we would actually succeed. I myself experienced one of those moments first hand.

On the way to where we would join John and the others to confront Henry, my men and I encountered Lord Clifford and his company of soldiers. They were in possession of strategically important equipment and supplies that were intended for Henry's use. Thankfully, we were able to overcome them, divest them of their valuable cargo, and thwart their ability to join Henry on the battlefield.

Regrettably, our luck would not last. We would ultimately be met with defeat. Sadly, any chance we had died along with the many brave souls who lost their lives that day. If I close my eyes, I can still see their bloodied bodies lying silent and dead upon the ground. All I can think is that they all died in vain. Such a waste. Such a pitiful horrifying waste. I wish I could go back in time and never agree to such a foolish endeavor. I wish I would have let things be.

But what if we had won? Would the boy have actually become king? Had we put an end to Henry, I would have eventually brought Edward's son out of hiding so he could rule.

Thanks to Henry's repeal of parliament's act declaring Edward's children to be illegitimate, Edward's son was now eligible to take the crown. However, I would have first had to convince everyone that he was not an imposter. Given that most people thought Lambert was George's heir, this would be no easy task. And no one, I might add, with the exception of myself, knew that any of Edward's sons were still alive.

You may ask, what did the others plan to do if we defeated Henry? Obviously, those who were unaware of the ruse fully expected Lambert to take the throne. I will have to admit that despite him having no legitimate right to the crown, he would have made a far better king than Henry.

As for the few who knew the truth about Lambert but had no knowledge of an alternative, honestly, they had no idea what they would do. I imagine they may have considered letting John rule had he survived, assuming he had any interest to take on such a burden. With the death of Richard's wife and child and a lack of a living heir, Richard knew it would be necessary to enter into another marriage to preserve the dynasty. However, if such a union could not be made or bear fruit, he strongly considered the potential of his nephew John succeeding him.

In reality, no one was truly resolute about who should take the crown had we been victorious. My fellow Yorkists were more concerned with first outing Henry and presumed they would figure things out once the deed was done. Again, not the best of plans.

But sometimes complacency and resignation seem far worse than acting blindly. Doing nothing may be too bitter a pill for people to swallow. Sometimes people need to do something, anything, even if there is a risk of failure and even death. All they can do is pray they hit the mark or come close enough for it to turn the tide.

Unfortunately, the only thing our efforts were able to achieve was to strengthen Henry's claim that he is our king and will continue to be our king. I pray that Henry has shown mercy to our boy pretender. It horrifies me to think of one so young having their life cut short or to suffer any pain. I feel sick just thinking about it.

17

HOW DID I GET HERE?

Now, dearest reader, I shall reward you for your tremendous patience with me, and reveal how I came to be where I am.

As you are aware, my final battle did not end in victory, but tragic defeat. Most of the people who fought beside me perished in our attempt to overthrow Henry. While things initially appeared to be in our favor, unfortunately, our odds of success swiftly plummeted against us. I imagine you may be wondering how I could survive, let alone escape, while others could not. Although the survival skills I developed early on were helpful, my continued living and freedom, if you could call it that, was in large part due to luck.

Just over two hours into the fighting, I felt as if I had been at it for days. My muscles burned and strained with every lift, swing and thrust I made with my sword. Every part of my body hurt even if I did not move. The fact that I was also injured and bleeding did not help. I knew I would not last much longer. Considering that I have never been much of a warrior, I was surprised that I lasted as long as I did.

As I took a moment to catch my breath and decide what to do, I could not help but stare at the carnage all around me. Tears, dirt and sweat blurred my vision but did not protect me from the horrific scene before my eyes.

Countless limbs, broken, twisted or sliced, blanketed the ground like branches and other debris after a storm. Torn flesh, vacant eyes, lives cut short met me every which way I turned. Friends and foes lay silently in pools of red, never to breathe, speak or fight again. Death was everywhere. I found it especially unsettling to look upon the dead Irish soldiers, who were so inadequately armored. Their bodies were stuck with so many arrows they reminded me of hedgehogs, bloody ones.

There was no sign of any of the men who accompanied me there, or anyone else I was personally acquainted with for that matter. I had no way to determine if they were dead or captured, or somehow able to flee. There only appeared to be a few German mercenaries and perhaps a few others I could not recognize still fighting against Henry's men.

It was clear that the battle was already lost and to stay and continue fighting would be futile. I had no desire to be captured and most likely tortured. Nor did I wish for my own body to join the other dead bodies strewn across the ground, even if my wound may have had other intentions. I saw no other option but to take my leave, as quietly, carefully and as quickly as I could.

My horse was gone. I had no other means to flee other than on foot. Although it would make my journey longer and more difficult and dangerous, I was determined to take my chances. I knew the river and reeds would provide the coverage I needed for my escape. After ensuring that no one was looking, I ducked into some brush and started to make my way along the swampy river's edge. I moved as quickly as I could, glancing back every few minutes to make certain that no one was following me.

Once I deemed I was far enough away, I divested myself of my armor and stripped down to just my shirt and breeches. This allowed me to move with less restriction, and of course less notice.

Thankfully, I still had in my possession a sword and a small knife should a need to defend myself arise. Unfortunately, the injuries and bruising I received from battle, along with the terrain I had to travel along, made my progress difficult. I also suspect they would have made any defensive action on my part less effective.

My right forearm still seared with pain from an injury I sustained when a stray halberd sliced through the air just a short time before. I tried desperately not to focus on the blood that still seeped from my wound and stained my shirt or the overwhelming weakness that racked my body. I was determined to keep moving but it was getting harder by the minute.

As I trudged through mud, water and brush, my boots felt like lead upon my feet. My muscles strained as I forced myself forward. Every step became an enormous effort on my part. Since, I had neither the luxury of time or safety on my side, I pressed on.

Aside from being alive and capable of moving, I had one critical advantage in my favor. I have long been familiar with the area I was traveling and knew exactly where to go for the best chance of avoiding discovery.

I knew the nearby woods would be the safest place to be, but I could not go there right away without risking being detected. So I would bide my time in the swampy river's edge until it was completely dark and then make my way into the woods.

I walked through the woods all night long until just before dawn. I eventually spotted a tiny village just a short distance beyond the woods. To my great fortune, I happened upon someone who was still loyal to the old king and willing to help me.

The kind man gave me food and water and tended as best as he could to my wounds. He also gave me a place to rest on his property. I made sure to keep a good distance away to avoid risking notice or endangering either my generous caretaker or myself.

I hid inside a hayrick that crisscrossed and was encircled with high brush. Its primary purpose was to shelter animals. But for a short time, it would also serve as my own shelter and temporary quarters.

Within the well protected boundaries of that simple yet vital structure, I would spend many a day trying to mend my body and regain some strength.

My makeshift housing and bed of hay had me thinking back upon my days at Middleham. It also had me longing for a good tale and the comforting reassurance of our dear ladies. I tried to imagine them standing there, urging me to get some rest as they draped a knitted blanket over my shoulders.

While there were no cozy blankets, calming voices or masterful storytellers to entertain or soothe my mind, I was grateful for having some place to lay my head. I did not even mind when an animal nuzzled up next to me to share warmth. It actually helped me to feel less alone and scared, especially at night when my mind overflowed with negative thoughts and images. These gentle creatures also served as a welcome distraction when the aches and pains in my body became more intense and more difficult to ignore.

When daylight broke each day, I would retreat into the nearby woods and remain there until sunset. Upon nightfall, I would once again return to the hayrick to gain shelter from the cooler air and darkness. I believed that shifting my location also made it safer for the people whose land served as my temporary haven.

After more than two weeks had passed since I took refuge there, I had begun to feel impatient for some news about Stoke and loathsome Henry. I wondered if any of the Yorkists had survived the battle and if so, what became of them. I was especially anxious to hear about our young Lambert.

Unfortunately, no one in that little village seemed to know anything. I assumed that the best information to be had would be in or near Stoke. Therefore, despite it being what many would call a bad idea, I decided to return to the location from where I escaped.

I know, dear reader, you must think me mad. I spent so much effort getting away without being captured and now I was determined to go back. I suspect you think even stubborn principled Richard would not risk returning to such a place. You are probably right. But honestly, I did not feel I had a choice.

Dressed in common peasant's attire, equipped with water and food and a few other supplies provided to me by my caretaker, I set off to find some answers. I began to make my way through the woods and head back to what remained of the battlefield. I did not know if I would see any of my fellow soldiers lingering about injured or dying when I got there, but I was determined to know either way.

Unfortunately, upon my arrival, I found no one, nor was I able to ascertain any information about the aftermath of the battle. Thankfully, as I suspected, Henry's men were long gone and there was no immediate danger. Regardless, I moved about as inconspicuously as possible and never let anyone know who I truly was.

In search of information and some rest, I decided to take shelter in a nearby monastery. The kindly priest and monks, with whom I sojourned, treated my injuries without question and told me I could stay as long as I wished.

I never revealed to them who I was, but I imagine it was not too difficult to conclude that I had fought at Stoke. I pretended to be less than my true station, and hoped the clothing I wore would strengthen the illusion. Despite that, I am sure they suspected due to my ability to write and read I was higher born than I made out to be.

I really did not need to worry about these Godly men alerting my enemy of my presence there. They were not there to judge, or get embroiled in political intrigue, nor would they ever consider doing something that would put themselves or me at risk. They desired only peace, contemplation and the ability to serve God.

Frustratingly though, the monks had absolutely no information to offer. It was as if the world outside went on without them. Other than being aware that some battle occurred not too long ago and not far from where they were, they were as uninformed about the goings on as anyone could be.

I recognized that if I wanted to discover the true state of things in the kingdom and determine how my fellow Yorkists had fared, I could not stay. Hence, after a month had passed, despite not being fully mended I took my leave.

I was determined to go to my family's home at Minster Lovell, where I hoped I still had some advocate or helper I could rely on for support. More importantly, I looked forward to the potential to acquire valuable information and make some plans.

Unfortunately, the journey from Stoke to Minster Lovell would be a long one, one that was fraught with danger. This was especially the case since the closer I got, the more likely I would encounter someone loyal to Henry. While I suspected my family's home was granted to one of Henry's supporters, I had no way of knowing for sure until I reached my destination. I also did not know what kind of circumstances would greet me upon my arrival.

I knew I was taking a huge risk going there, but as I previously mentioned, I really believed it would be the last place they would expect me to turn up.

While I would occasionally have the opportunity to ride upon a peasant cart for short distances, unfortunately most of my journey would be on foot. Unsurprisingly, it took an exceedingly long time to get here. As a result, whatever strength and energy I managed to reclaim during my time with the monks was sapped greatly on my way home.

When I arrived at my destination, I was relieved to discover there were a number of people still residing at Minster Lovell who I knew and trusted. And while it could put them all at risk, they were more than willing to help me.

Although food and other resources were in short supply, these generous souls shared what they had without hesitation. As for information, there was little they could tell me initially. However, they were more than willing to gather what they could. I needed all the information I could get to figure out what to do next and ensure that I did not get caught or endanger anyone else in the process. I had no doubt that my clever and resourceful group of helpers were up to the challenge.

As I mentioned before, my family's estate is currently granted to Henry's uncle Jasper. Fortunately for me and the people who live and work here, Jasper is off away on some business for his nephew king. This certainly makes it better for my safety, but it also spares the people who live here from having to deal with someone they do not like. It is not because he is a Tudor, even though being one does not work in his favor. He is simply an unlikable sort of person. At least that is what I have heard.

Clearly, most people around here would be much happier if he would just stay away. Time will tell if he will return or find another place that suits him better. But as long as he is gone, the remaining inhabitants of Minster Lovell are breathing a sigh of relief, as am I.

Having Jasper out of the way, even temporarily, was something I did not count on, but viewed as a positive sign that things might be turning in my favor. While that in itself could be considered sufficient reason for me to stay where I was, there was even more good news welcoming me upon my arrival.

Surprisingly, Jasper left only a sparse number of his men behind to guard the property in his absence. As such, it is quite easy to move about without being bothered or detected. Despite that, I choose to spend

most of my time in this hidden chamber. In the event
that Tudor's guards decide to conduct a random
search of the house and grounds, or Jasper makes an
unannounced visit, no one will find me. Nor will
they discover any trace of my being here.

The chamber in which I spend most of my hours
is furnished with a bed, a large wooden table and two
fairly comfortable high backed chairs. There is even a
privy of sorts conveniently located in one corner of the
room. The hole, which extends deep into the ground,
is cleverly enclosed in a box like structure to prevent
odors from escaping into the rest of the space.

My caretakers have provided me with a number of
comforts and necessities including blankets, candles,
writing paper and implements, maps, a book,
clothing, and most importantly water and food.

Someone comes to my chamber every few days to
check on the state of my health, and deliver food or
other supplies and any information they have
gathered. To throw off any suspicion and prevent
someone from noticing a pattern that could lead to
my discovery, they are careful to vary the times of
their visits. My loyal group of helpers also frequently
alternate among themselves as to who comes to see me
and when.

When Minster Lovell was initially built, the master of the house requested that the chamber in which I currently reside be constructed in secret. He wanted to have a safe place for him and his family to go should the unimaginable occur. During those early days, the chamber was regularly stocked with a variety of supplies and items to provide for the family's comfort and needs.

Many years later, when my grandfather William purchased the estate, he engaged the services of builders and craftsman to construct a much finer manor house than the original one. Because he saw the value in having the chamber, he was careful to preserve its existence and secrecy and had the workers build around it.

Very few people have been privy to its presence over the years. Thankfully, my father told me about it not long before he died. It was actually a couple days before he was going off to fight yet another battle.

"Francis," he said in his most serious voice and with the most solemn of expressions on his face, "you will be the man of the house when I leave. Should something happen, I am counting on you to take care of your mother and sister."

"If any of you are truly in peril," he added, "I want you to know there is a secret chamber at Minster Lovell where you can hide until the danger has passed. While there are some supplies already there, you will have to bring more items with you should the need arise."

He then proceeded to explain in detail how to get to the chamber and revealed how it was connected to a room in the main house. The room of which I speak is located directly above the chamber. Rarely occupied by family, servants or guests, the space is primarily used for storage.

The two rooms are connected to allow air to flow into the chamber. Air comes through four large holes that were cut into all four corners of the chamber's ceiling, as well as the floor of the spare room above. The openings in the room upstairs are concealed behind ornately carved decorative panels designed to prevent their detection.

Because sound can travel up and down through the holes in the chamber, I am careful not to make too much noise. It is a particular concern when I am not alone. Thus, I have committed to only speaking in hushed tones when I have visitors. As a further precaution, my helpers post someone in the vicinity of the upstairs room during visits to ensure that none of Jasper's men are able to overhear our conversations.

The holes shared by the chamber and the room above offer an added benefit of being a way to pass messages and other small items I might require. This allowed me to have something in my possession much more quickly and easily than having it delivered in person. These openings also provided a means to let some needed light into the chamber, beyond what is generated by my candles, that is.

Sparse amount of light, combined with occasional sounds from up above helped me to feel less isolated or trapped. But when I felt I could not bear to spend one more second in such confined quarters, I would slip outside briefly for some fresh air and sunshine.

Knowing the predictable daily movements of Jasper's men was exceedingly helpful in facilitating my rare and wonderful moments of freedom. I would have liked to wander the grounds more often, but I was not willing to risk my discovery or the safety of my loyal helpers.

18

FAREWELL DEAR DIARY

Dearest diary, I have spent the last forty nine days hoping and praying, while trying to gain strength, make plans and come to terms with my life. I have occupied many of those days writing in your pages, my side of a story that I fear will never be heard. Despite that, I had absolutely no choice but to tell it.

I have placed you in a large leather pouch and hidden you in a secret opening behind a stone in the wall that lines this very chamber. I fear that if you should be found too quickly, good people would be in danger. Therefore, hidden you shall stay, at least for now.

I have only told three people of your existence. They have all committed to keeping this knowledge a secret, until such time they perceive it to be safe to reveal your contents. Sadly, I have little hope that day will ever come.

In the event my wonderful, kind and loyal helpers discover me dead, I have instructed them to leave my body where they found it. I do not want them to jeopardize their own lives to bury me. They were also reminded to seal up the holes connecting the chamber and the manor, to ensure that no smells from my decaying body reach the main living area. I urged them to tell no one that I was ever here and trust them completely to do as I have asked. I pray they will be kept safe and that their deeds will remain unknown to everyone except God and myself.

I am afraid my time with you, dear reader, is nearing its end. While my injuries have all mended, I have never been able to overcome the pervasive weakness that has racked my body since fleeing from Stoke. Regrettably, I become weaker by the day and any hope for the future is dimming rapidly. My health is failing. I know I will not live much longer.

My lungs have become inflamed and congested, making it difficult to breathe. I can barely speak or move without coughing. I am also miserably feverish. My body temperature changes swiftly by the moment. I alternate from feeling as though I may never cease shivering, to burning with such heat, I fear I will burst into flames and end up a pile of ash. My appetite and ability to eat what little food is available is nonexistent. I cannot sleep, yet I am desperately tired. It is also painfully clear that my body is too weak to get better.

I am trying desperately not to succumb to bitterness in my final days, but I am feeling very angry at the moment.

There are many reasons for my anger. I am angry at the injustices in this world, where ego, disloyalty, incompetence and greed are rewarded. I am angry with my body for failing me and causing me to suffer. I am angry at my bloody stubbornness and foolishness in continuing to fight for something that was lost long ago. I am angry for having much of my life dictated by the whims of others. I am angry for not being able to have the life I wanted. But most of all, I am angry that I will never have the new beginning I have hoped and planned for.

I have prayed to the Lord Almighty to lift this anger from my heart. I hope he is not too busy to hear me and is willing to aid me in my time of difficulty. In the meantime, I have chosen to spend my last moments focusing on more positive thoughts.

As I look upon my life, however badly things might have turned out, there are some things I am grateful for and even proud of. I have tried to do my best at whatever responsibility was thrust upon me and uphold a sense of value and honor in a less than honorable world. I have experienced great friendship in a time and place that valued material wealth and title above matters of the heart or loyalty. While I did not have as many adventures as I would have liked, I am thankful for the ones I had.

Although I have not had much to be cheerful about in a long time, I do cherish the happy times and laughs I did have. I am also honored and humbled by the kindness shown to me by people who have not always been treated as kindly. I will always hold a special place in my heart for each and every one of them. I pray for God's mercy and blessing to lighten their hearts and lives and protect them in this dangerous world.

As I write these words, I suddenly find myself thinking about my mother. She died only a couple years after my father, while I was at Middleham. The years we had together were so few. The times we shared together were even fewer. However, there is one memory that I have long forgotten that stands out among all others.

In that brief moment in time, I saw my mother in a way that I never saw before or would ever see again. For some strange reason, this memory is now running through my head as clear as if it were yesterday. Although I am surprised to be thinking about it after all these years, I am grateful for the comfort it is now giving me.

I was about five years old at the time. I do not recall what upset me, but I was nevertheless close to being inconsolable. Curled almost into a ball, I sat there alone crying hysterically for what seemed like forever.

Before I thought I would drown in my own tears, my typically unemotional and unaffectionate mother suddenly came into the room and took a seat beside me. She reached her arms around me and put me on her lap. Her hand gently brushed the hair away from my face so that my tear filled eyes could see her own.

"Hush now, it will be alright," she said in soothing tones as she rocked me and stroked my hair, "you will be alright."

I blinked twice, as if the act would somehow help me confirm that I was not dreaming and that all of this was real. I found myself suddenly feeling calmer and even happy as my mother continued to hold me in her arms and reassure me. After embracing me for quite a long time, she then posed a question to me.

"Do you know why you are named Francis?" she asked. I shook my head and rubbed at my eyes in response.

"I shall tell you," she said with the sweetest of smiles on her face. "I was feeling very desperate and despaired you see," she began.

This really piqued my curiosity. I could not imagine my mother ever feeling such a thing. I stared into her eyes eagerly anticipating what she might say.

"I wanted a child," she explained, "but to my continued sorrow, God had not blessed me with one. I prayed every day in hopes that he would grant me my heart's desire, but my prayers were not answered. Then one day, I was sitting in contemplation in a chapel when a painting of Saint Francis caught my eye. His face looked particularly kind and his eyes very sympathetic. I suddenly felt compelled to speak to the painting, as if doing so would allow the real Saint Francis to hear me."

"Saint Francis, I said, I need your help. I wish to have a baby, preferably a boy. But I would also be happy with a girl. Please, I begged him, please give me a baby. If you do this, I promise I will name my son or daughter after you and honor you for the rest of my life."

"I had the strangest sense of peace and hope wash over me after making my request. Somehow, I knew Saint Francis heard me and wanted to help. Then just a few short months later, I discovered that I was pregnant. When you were born, I fulfilled my promise and named you Francis to show my gratitude. You my dearest son are my miracle. No matter how bad things may seem to be, always remember that something can happen to make it alright."

Honestly, I was speechless. I never felt so special in my entire life as I did at that moment. With all the pain, disappointment and loneliness I have experienced in my life, I forgot all about that wonderful moment so long ago. I forgot that I was wanted. And despite my mother not being able to show her affection on a regular basis, I know she loved me in the best way she could.

Now as I leave this earth, I know God has granted me my own prayer. I shall not leave with anger or bitterness. I shall leave in peace. I feel peace in knowing that I lived toward an ideal, which I did my best to bring into reality. More importantly, I have peace in the realization that I mattered.

I recognize now that I was not really alone, even though the people in my life could not be there for me the way I wanted. Although people are not always equipped to help us in our daily life, sometimes they can surprise us when we need them most. With this thought, I leave with a final gift from my mother, knowing that I will be alright.

I do thank you, my devoted reader, for indulging my need to blabber on as I have, and bid you the best of luck and good wishes. I look forward to closing my eyes and seeing my boyhood friend once again. It comforts me to think of him happily reunited with his beloved wife and son these past years. I truly hope he is well rested and back to his joyful self, for I am impatient for some new adventures.

Yours truly,

Francis Lovell -- Woof!

I have one more thing to add. If Henry Tudor is still alive, I pray that he does not stay that way too long and that a more honorable man takes his place on the throne. At the very least, it would make me ever so happy if his prick suddenly shriveled up and fell off, ensuring that he will never know any more pleasure. If the latter happens prior to his leaving this world, I would be doubly grateful.

AUTHOR'S NOTE

I t's easy to get lost in the sea of names, dates, military engagements and other historical details on which those who study history tend to focus. While it is certainly important to know what and when things occurred in the past, it is the people who lived through these times and events that attract more of my attention.

By delving into the thoughts, feelings and motivations of those who were part of history, one can get a glimpse behind the curtain, if you will. That rare insight that gives more personal meaning to history. And then just maybe, people can learn from those who came before them and make choices that create a better future.

While very little is known about Francis Lovell, what is clear to numerous people including myself, is that he was a loyal and true friend, even beyond death. Because those attributes were uncommon for the times he lived in, it's easy to see why there is a great deal of curiosity regarding this elusive historical figure. Many conjecture about how he became one of the most powerful men in England, serving a king who would be maligned for over five hundred years.

The recent discovery of King Richard III's bones has sparked a renewed interest in his life and times. It has reignited an ongoing and heated debate about the alleged history to which Richard is tied.

He was the last English king to die in battle. His victors defiled his body upon death and set out to tarnish his name and reputation. Many years later, William Shakespeare would write a play that would ensure that this king would forever be viewed as a monster. Yet ironically, more than five hundred years after Richard's death, thousands of people would line the streets of England to celebrate and pay last respects to him. They watched on with excitement and sometimes reverence as his remains made their way to their final and more proper resting place.

Finding Richard would also provide an added bonus of generating millions of dollars of tourism-related income for the city of Leicester, where his skeleton was uncovered. Many even believe giving this king a proper burial also ended a longstanding losing streak for Leicester's premier soccer league team. Righting their karmic debt is also given credit for securing them a championship win for the first time in the club's history. What a humorous and ironic twist that a man who history viewed as a villain could now be considered a good luck charm.

On a more serious note, the heightened attention and interest Richard is receiving has spurred more questions and has revealed more evidence to challenge the world's view of him. It is becoming even more apparent that the largely propaganda driven history about him has a lot of holes and inconsistencies. Hopefully it will soon be seen for what it is and the truth will prevail.

In revisiting and questioning the past as it relates to this controversial king, one could not help but think about his key associates. Most significantly, people wonder about the man who worked alongside of him and continued fighting after his friend and king was dead.

There is much speculation about what Francis was really like and how he could have remained loyal to someone whom history regarded so unfavorably. But more than anything, people are curious about what became of him.

Some asserted that he did not survive his last attempt to kill Henry Tudor despite his body never being found. More than a few claimed Francis had escaped alive, but was wounded and not expected to live much longer. Others had him living out his days in Scotland or some other place beyond the reach of his enemy king.

Scotland's King James IV was said to have issued a grant of safe conduct to several exiled Yorkists including Lovell about a year after Stoke. However, other than a random rumor about someone that looked like him being spotted outside of England many years later, there is no evidence to prove this to be true.

However, one of the more dramatic theories regarding Francis' end had him trapped and dying of starvation in a chamber beneath one of his family's estates. The assumption was that he accidently locked himself in and had no means of escape. It was believed that either no one knew he was there in the first place or that his lone servant died and was unable to return to rescue him.

Of all the potential scenarios to explain his disappearance after his last known sighting at the battle of Stoke, the chamber made the most sense to me, with some exceptions. I did not believe he was trapped or that he starved to death. I also never bought into the idea that no one knew he was there.

When Minster Lovell was undergoing renovations in the early 1700s, it was said that workers discovered a hidden chamber with bones and other items as I described in my prologue. Unfortunately, no one is able to prove this or say what happened to said bones or if there were any words written on the pages they allegedly found.

Most people think it is a ridiculous notion that Francis would have returned to a place where he could have easily been discovered and where they believe he no longer had any supporters. But I could see the logic where others could not.

No one can avoid detection and punishment for two years and help coordinate a rebellion without incredible instincts and a loyal following. Bonds made over time are not forgotten or broken just because a person disappears for a while, especially when circumstances are beyond their control. Moreover, Henry would never suspect that Lovell would have the audacity to return to a home that was gifted to one of his enemies. Therefore, it really would be the perfect place for Francis to bide his time.

And if he had a secret chamber in which he could hide, all the better.

I tried to imagine how he got there and why, along with what he might have written if he had the opportunity before he died. This book is the diary I believe Francis would have composed if he could. One final chance to tell his side of the story before it was too late. While doing so would not change anything, it could provide a cathartic release from all the trauma he experienced and perhaps give him some measure of peace in the end. For a future reader, it would be a rare glimpse into the mindset and hearts of two friends burdened with responsibility, all the while facing constant adversity and danger.

The times and lives of King Richard III and his mysterious sidekick Francis Lovell incite many arguments among historians. With an overabundance of negative political propaganda, along with insufficient and conflicting historical documentation, there is no way to definitively prove anyone's case.

However, if Francis' last written words did exist and could be found, it could shake up the whole historical community and maybe even bring the arguments to an end. The potential to clear up every mystery and misconception surrounding this maligned king once and for all would be an exciting draw for any historical sleuth or truth seeker.

It is striking to me how little is known of Francis' life and whereabouts, except for a few impersonal details like property holdings, titles and ancestry. Every now and then, the rare personal tidbit may surface. However, it is most likely of questionable authenticity or generally adds little to nothing in helping us understand him better.

Francis was in one of the most powerful positions in government and was one of the wealthiest landowners at the time. Yet oddly, he carried on his life leaving nothing behind and without anyone taking note of it. References to him are so rare, books regarding the time in which he lived barely mention him or frequently have to make something up because no one really knows. Even his birth date is unknown.

Anyone wanting to know more about him is destined to find a cold trail and a pile of rumors and assumptions. I cannot help but think that he intended to be invisible. Given the state of things, I could see how that might be helpful.

Francis' ability to hide in plain sight and elude capture and death for so long when others could not is particularly fascinating to me. This man clearly knew how to work the system and understood people so well, he could anticipate what they might do and use it to his advantage. A testament to his extraordinary talent for survival has surfaced in modern day in an unusual way that I would like to share with you.

When researching Francis, I discovered that he was made a knight in the Order of Garter in 1483. Although I have heard of this organization before, I really did not know very much about it. This highly prestigious chivalric-based order was formed in the mid 1300s by King Edward III. Its founding is thought to be an homage to the Knights of the Round Table in Arthurian legend.

Each knight in the order is designated a personal stall in St. George's Chapel in Windsor Castle, where upon a brass plate containing their name and arms is hung. If a knight of the Garter was convicted of treason or considered unworthy for some reason, he was ejected from the order by a process called degradation. When this occurred, among many things, the former knight would be subjected to public humiliation and his stall plate would be removed and destroyed.

Because Francis did not pledge loyalty to King Henry VII, he was considered a traitor to the crown.

As such, all his properties and wealth were attainted and he was stripped of all titles and honors bestowed upon him. Obviously, this included his removal from the Order of the Garter. Here's the strange part. His Garter plate was never destroyed. It hangs in St. George's Chapel as I write this. There is no explanation as to why it survived when others did not.

I can only surmise that Henry put off any actions regarding the plate until he could obtain definitive confirmation of Francis' death or continued existence. I can't see him wasting an opportunity to shame and minimize one of the last remnants of Richard III's power structure, let alone dearest friend. I suspect as time went on, Henry simply forgot about it.

As a symbol of Francis' honorable qualities and fortitude, I chose to proudly display his enduring Garter plate image on my book cover.

As for the contents of my book, known and true information is intertwined with a great deal of supposition on my part. Obviously, there is no way for me to prove my theories and assumptions about this man. However, my study and understanding of human behavior makes me believe that what I have imagined may be a lot closer to the truth than one might think.

I know that I have detoured from many of the prevailing assumptions about Richard and Francis, even those widely accepted by Ricardians. But when I decided to write the book, I was determined to view these men, their experiences and potential motivations with a different lens. My objective was simply to create new dialogues and just maybe help bring more truth to light.

I hope what I have written has offered you potential explanations and understandings that will allow you to view Richard III and the time in which he lived with fresh new eyes. Most of all, I hope you have enjoyed getting to know my take on the elusive Francis Lovell, one of history's most loyal friends and unsung heroes.

I actually have one more thing to talk about that has nothing to do with Francis but everything to do with Richard.

Other than being remembered for being the inspiration for a villain in a Shakespearian play, most people minimize the significance of Richard III's brief time on the throne. Historians often understate the enlightened legislation this king put into place. They also pay little note to how history itself might have been very different and perhaps better had Richard not died. I truly believe that the end of his reign and life was a proverbial fork in the road, even though most people don't see it that way.

Had Henry VII been killed instead of Richard, Henry VIII would not have existed. Corruption, excessive violence and executions, disempowerment and dishonor were hallmarks of this infamous king's rule and continued with future Tudors. More significantly, his reworking of the church and intolerance for other religious perspectives set in motion conflicts that would persist for hundreds of years.

Changing one's religion to something that is more supportive of their choices and lifestyle is perfectly understandable. Coercing everyone else to change with you or suffer the consequences is not.

Henry's small mindedness and desperation for control and power cost many people their lives and livelihood. It allowed bitterness and hatred to take root. Though Henry VIII is long gone from this world, his country and the ones that surround it are still in the process of healing the wounds he inflicted.

The my-religion-is-better-than-your-religion-so-change-or-die mentality has fueled arguments and triggered bloodshed from the moment humans attempted to understand their circumstances by giving it a spiritual framework. Therefore, there is no guarantee that future disagreements or even war could have been prevented had the Tudors never ruled. However, I suspect this world would have experienced less divisiveness and corruption and been a much better place had Richard lived. Just Sayin'. ☺

ABOUT THE AUTHOR

Dawn Wheeler is a Certified Hypnotherapist and author who also happens to like history. Upon hearing of the discovery of King Richard III's bones, she set out to find more information about why Richard was so controversial. In delving into this much maligned king's story, she learned of a man who worked alongside of him who was uncharacteristically loyal. Francis Lovell's mysterious life and disappearance, as well as the legends that attempt to explain it, captured Dawn's curiosity. With her understanding of human behavior, she was also drawn to examine his motivations and actions and reconcile her own assessments against prevailing opinions. Despite the unusually sparse information available, she was determined to tell his story. Dawn currently resides in Michigan with her husband. She hopes one day of visiting the ruins of Minster Lovell where Francis is rumored to have taken his last breath and where her book takes place.